Dead
Giveaway

By the same author:

CAST, IN ORDER OF DISAPPEARANCE
SO MUCH BLOOD
STAR TRAP
AN AMATEUR CORPSE
A COMEDIAN DIES
THE DEAD SIDE OF THE MIKE
SITUATION TRAGEDY
MURDER UNPROMPTED
MURDER IN THE TITLE
NOT DEAD, ONLY RESTING
A SHOCK TO THE SYSTEM
TICKLED TO DEATH

Dead Giveaway

Simon Brett

CHARLES SCRIBNER'S SONS
NEW YORK

First published in the United States
by Charles Scribner's Sons 1986

Copyright © 1985 Simon Brett

Library of Congress Cataloging-in-Publication Data

Brett, Simon.
  Dead giveaway.

  I. Title.
PR6052.R4296D38   1986   823'.914   85-18407
ISBN 0-684-18517-2

Printed in the United States of America.

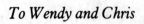

To Wendy and Chris

Chapter One

"MR . . . PARIS DID you say?"

"Yes."

The girl on the desk at West End Television's main Reception looked dubiously down at a list. Charles Paris's name didn't seem to leap out of the page at her.

"For what show did you say?"

"*If The Cap Fits.*"

This title did not dispel her scepticism. "No show of that name down on my list."

"It's a pilot of a new game show. Something to do with hats."

"Hats. Ah." Comprehension dawned slowly. "That might be what I've got down here as *Hats Off!*"

"It could be. Maybe the title's been changed. As I say, it is only a pilot. Studio A," Charles added helpfully.

"Yes, that's where *Hats Off!*'s booked in." The girl was forced, regretfully, to accept his *bona fides*. "All right. If you like to sit down over there, someone will be down shortly."

"Thank you."

Charles started towards the low upholstered sofa she had indicated, when the girl's voice stopped him. "That is, unless you're one of the celebrities. If you are, they'll send someone down specially."

He turned to look at her.

"No," she said. "No, of course not. You go and sit and wait over there."

He had to confess it hurt. Charles Paris was not an actor

7

with an excessive amount of pride, but to have his non-celebrity status identified so immediately was a little galling. It rubbed in the humiliation of his very presence at West End Television that afternoon. As his agent, Maurice Skellern, had told him with considerable glee, the booking had only been made late the previous day.

"Just had a call from W.E.T.," Maurice had announced over the phone.

"Oh yes?" Charles had replied eagerly. The shock of his agent's actually ringing him had given way to exciting fantasies of leading parts in long-running television series.

"They're doing this new game show."

"Really?" The fantasies shifted to produce a new, suave Charles Paris on a panel of celebrities, quipping away with the best of them.

"Yes. Thing is, one of the rounds they have people from different professions and the contestants have to guess what they do from what they look like."

"Oh?"

"For reasons best known to themselves, they want one of the people to be an actor."

"Ah."

"Obviously, though, they can't run the risk of having a face the punters are going to recognize."

"No."

"So they rang me to see if I'd got any actors on my books who the public were very unlikely to have seen."

"Oh."

"I thought of you immediately, Charles."

Some actors might have reacted to this backhanded insult, some put the phone down, some bawled out their agent, many turned down the job. But Charles had been in the business too long, and been out of work too long, to afford such luxuries as pride. A job was a job. He'd agreed to participate.

The sofa on which he sat was extravagantly low, in keeping with the glamour of television. It was also extravagantly uncomfortable. It might have been all right for someone lying flat on his back, but any normal-sized adult trying to sit on it had to fold like a bank-note. Charles looked at the other people waiting in similar discomfort on similar sofas, and wondered whether any of them was involved in *If The Cap Fits*. Maybe they too were representatives of professions which had to be identified from their appearance. He tried to play the game, and came up with a bank cashier, an estate agent, a professional footballer, a dental nurse and a test pilot. But he didn't feel confident that he had scored very highly.

One of the lifts swished open and a girl emerged. She wore a khaki flying-suit, the television uniform of that autumn, and carried that symbol of television authority, a clipboard. Her hair was cut in the rigid shape of a crash-helmet and dyed the colour of copper beech. Her poise was daunting.

The pale-blue eyes went straight to the girl at the Reception desk, who nodded with something not far removed from contempt towards the sofas. The pale-blue eyes flickered upwards in a gesture of mock-prayer before joining her mouth in a professional smile as the girl moved towards her quarries.

"Good afternoon. Which ones of you are for *If The Cap Fits?*"

Charles, two other men and one girl rose with difficulty from their sofas. He'd been wrong about the estate agent and the test pilot, who did not stir.

"Hello. Welcome to West End Television. My name's Sydnee Danson."

Why, thought Charles, not for the first time, why do girls in television always have silly names?

"I'm one of the researchers on *If The Cap Fits*. The producer and everyone else is delighted that you've all agreed

9

to take part in the show, and we think you're really going to have a fun day. If you like to follow me, we'll go down to the studio and then you'll see what you have to do."

A certain amount of mutual introduction and feeble joking ensued as the four followed the unnerving Sydnee to the lift doors. She pressed the button to go down, then looked back for another covert (but not quite covert enough to be unseen by Charles) grimace of mock-despair to her friend on Reception.

Her expression changed sharply as she saw someone coming through the main doors. "Quick," she hissed, like a demented sheepdog, hustling her charges towards a door marked "EMERGENCY STAIRS". "In here!"

They scrambled through in confusion and found themselves on a small concrete landing. Sydnee leant panting against the door after she had closed it.

"Sorry," she replied to the four quizzical expressions. "That was one of the contestants coming in. They mustn't see you till the show or the game's ruined."

"What, so you've got to keep us apart all afternoon?"

"Yes," said Sydnee, and then added without great enthusiasm, "That's my job."

The set for *If The Cap Fits* was a geometric confusion of red, blue and silver. Against the backdrop tall triangles of blue provided an Alpine horizon, in front of which was mounted a wheel of red, around whose perimeter the title *If The Cap Fits* was picked out in large letters of silver. Another blue triangle, this time tapering downwards, provided a lectern in the centre of the area, and to one side a long rectangular blue desk was set in front of four red chairs. On the desk were four red-and-blue-striped drinking glasses; another stood on the lectern beside a red-and-blue-striped carafe. Across the front of the desk and of the lectern the show's name was again printed in silver, lest the viewing public should at any time forget which programme they were watching (a very real danger in the world of game shows).

As Sydnee ushered her four "professions" into the studio, a young man with a raven-black Mohican haircut and black leather bondage-suit was anxiously checking the spin of the red wheel. Over the studio loudspeakers a jingle was playing. Falsetto voices at high speed sang the deathless lyric,

> *If the cap fits,*
> *If the cap fits,*
> *If the cap FITS!*

The noise was, to Charles's mind, nauseating. But the jingle, and the set, raised interesting questions about the show's title. "It is called *If The Cap Fits* then?" he asked Sydnee, who was standing at his side.

She turned her incurious pale-blue eyes at him. "What?"

"The show is called *If The Cap Fits*?"

"Yes. Of course it is."

"At Reception they said something about *Hats Off!*"

"Ah, that's the title of the American version. There was some thought of keeping that for here . . . until quite recently."

"Not very recently."

"What do you mean?" For the first time there was a glint of mild interest in her eye.

"Well, it must have taken time to get the set built and the music recorded."

"Yes." She nodded slowly, recognizing with a degree of surprise that she was talking to someone who knew a little about television. For a second Charles saw in her eyes that there might be a real person somewhere behind her professional exterior.

The moment passed as she raised her voice to address her charges.

"This is the set where you'll be performing. Shortly you'll be meeting the show's host. . . ."

"Oh, who is it?" asked the one female in the party.

"Barrett Doran."

"Ooh," she intoned with a wide-eyed giggle. "My lucky day. I think he's dead sexy."

To Charles, who was not a student of television game shows, the name meant nothing.

Sydnee continued her routine. "You'll actually be standing over here when you do your bit, which is incidentally in the First Round. . . ." She led the little group across the floor towards a blue-and-silver-striped flat. The black-leather Mohican turned as they passed. His face was white and anxious.

"This is Sylvian, who's designed the set."

"Ooh, well done, Sylvian," said the one female in the party. "It's really lovely."

The designer gave a twitchy nod in reaction to the compliment and turned back to his red wheel.

Before Sydnee could give more instructions, her attention was caught by the entry of a dumpy woman with blonded hair, on whose contours a khaki flying-suit hung less flatteringly. The new arrival carried not only a clipboard, but also a stopwatch, suggesting that her authority was that of a Producer's Assistant. She gave an imperious gesture and Sydnee scuttled across towards her.

A whispered conference ensued, and the researcher returned with her professional smile screwed back in place. "I'm sorry. I'm afraid Barrett won't actually be able to come down to the studio for the moment, but the Executive Producer, John Mantle, should be along shortly and. . . ."

She stopped on another gesture from the dumpy woman and crossed over for another quick whisper. "No, I'm sorry," Sydnee apologised as she returned, "John Mantle's still tied up in . . . er, an important meeting, but the

Producer, Jim Trace-Smith, will be here in a minute and he'll be able to brief you. Meanwhile, perhaps we ought to sort out the actual hats that you'll be wearing for the show." Pitching her voice up, she called to the studio in general, "Is there anyone from Wardrobe around?"

Her plea produced a tired-looking girl in a silver flying-suit and a limp-looking bald man in a pink flying-suit.

"I wondered if you'd sorted out the hats for the First Round . . . ?" asked Sydnee with diplomatic diffidence.

"More or less," the girl replied, and then revealed the reason for the researcher's tentative approach. "But we're still not happy about it. I mean, Wardrobe is about costumes that people *wear*. Hats for a game show I'd still have said come under Props."

"Yes, I see your point, but the hats are actually going to be *worn*," Sydnee cajoled. "These people here are going to wear them."

The girl's sniff showed that she remained unconvinced. "Well, I've talked to Head of Wardrobe and she says we should do it for today—under protest, mind—but if the show goes to a series, alternative arrangements may well have to be made."

"Yes, yes," the researcher agreed readily. "Let's cross that bridge when we come to it. But can we see what you've got for us today?"

The bald man in the pink flying-suit was grudgingly despatched, and soon came back with a selection of hat-boxes. "But we would like to make it clear that we're still not happy about it," he insisted.

"Yes, I understand." Sydnee reached eagerly towards the boxes.

"Do you mind?" said the girl shirtily. "You're not Wardrobe, are you?"

"No."

"Well, handling hats is a Wardrobe job."

"Yes, of course." Sydnee withdrew, her poise momentarily threatened, while the girl from Wardrobe demanded, "Right, who wants what?"

Sydnee stepped forward again. "Now you see, each one of them has to wear a hat which symbolizes his or her profession. Did you get the list of professions?"

"No," the girl replied stonily.

"Well, Charles Paris here, for instance, is an actor . . ."

"Oh yes?" The girl in silver battle-dress reached into a box, pulled out a floppy Tudor bonnet and thrust it at Charles. "Try that."

He put it on. It was too big. "I'm not sure that this actually says 'actor' . . ." he began.

"That," the girl hissed in a voice that brooked no disagreement, "is what actors wear. That is your hat. That is what you will wear. You are now responsible for it. You will look after it. You will see that no one else wears it."

"Ah," said Charles. "Right."

"Erm . . ." Sydnee interposed. "I'm afraid that won't quite work. You see, the point of the game is that they don't wear their right hats."

The girl from Wardrobe looked at her pityingly.

"No, you see, they have to wear the wrong hats, and it's up to the punters—er, the contestants to change them round and get them wearing the right ones. That's why the game's called what it's called. *If The Cap Fits*," Sydnee concluded lamely.

"Look, you wanted hats to fit four people. Now you tell me you don't want them to fit those four people—they've got to fit four other people. What is going on?"

"No, they're not meant to fit four other specific people. The contestants may move them around. They're meant to fit any of them . . . all four of them."

The girl from Wardrobe folded her arms over her silver flying-suit. Her tired mouth took on an even harder line. "I am not in Wardrobe to supply hats that don't fit. I am trained to supply costumes that do fit."

Sydnee looked fazed. It was not clear how she was going to get out of this one. But, before she could attempt any solution, her eye caught movement at the side of the studio and was once again lit up by sudden panic. "Quick, quick!" she cried. "Someone's bringing the contestants in! Come on—this way!"

And again she did her sheepdog routine, bundling the four "professions" out of Studio A.

Sydnee's party came through double doors out of Studio A and started up the corridor which led towards the lifts. As they approached, the lift doors opened and their leader saw something which made her reverse promptly, shepherding her flock back the way they had come.

"What was it?"

"Just getting out of the lift. Nick Jeffries."

"Ooh," squealed the one female in the party. "You mean Nick Jeffries, the boxer?"

"Yes. He's on the panel for the show."

"Ooh, you've got all the sexy ones on, haven't you? Did you select them. EH?"

This last was accompanied by a huge nudge to Sydnee, who offered hardly even a pretence of a smile in return. Then she looked behind her and saw, to her horror, a bulky man in a plush sheepskin jacket following them down the corridor. "It's Nick Jeffries," she gasped. "Quick, in here!"

She thrust open the nearest door, over which a sign read, "STUDIO B. AUTHORISED PERSONNEL ONLY."

They found themselves in darkness, cramped between a wall and a loose hanging curtain. "Follow me," urged Sydnee. They followed. Rounding the corner of the curtain, the five of them were momentarily blinded by the sudden glare of studio lights.

The set in Studio B was considerably smaller than that in Studio A. (Indeed, the whole studio was smaller.) It represented a study-like room, a cross between a barrister's chambers and an amateur laboratory. Shelves of leather-bound books encased the walls, while the surfaces were littered with a variety of phials and retorts. Firearms, daggers and the occasional skull had been scattered in calculated disorder. The set could have been designed for an updated remake of Sherlock Holmes.

And, though the man at the centre of this space could not have been mistaken for the great detective, he was, as it happened, speaking of crime. "And here we have it—" he was saying, in an exaggerated French accent, indicating a small elegantly-shaped bottle with a glass stopper which he held between thumb and forefinger, "perhaps the quickest-acting of all poisons. Cyanide. Beloved of detective-story writers, though significantly less popular with real murderers. Cyanide can kill in as little as ten seconds. Well, though I said it is not popular with murderers, there have still been one or two juicy cases where it was the favoured method. In 1907 Richard Brinkley. . . ."

"Ooh, it's Melvyn Gasc," hissed the one female in the party, peering at the speaker beyond the cameras. "He did that series on torture, didn't he?"

"This is the follow-up," Sydnee hissed back. "It's called *Method In Their Murders*. Being made for Channel Four."

"What are you doing here?" a third female voice hissed. Charles could make out a shapely outline in a flying-suit of indeterminate colour which had stepped in between his group and the light.

"Chippy. It's me, Sydnee. I'm trying to keep this lot out of the way. Mustn't be seen by the others in this game show."

"Barrett's thing?"

"Yes."

"Has the Great Shit himself put in an appearance yet?"

"He's around."

"Maybe I should go and have a word with him . . ."

"No, Chippy. This show's going to be hectic enough without that kind of complication."

"I don't know. I'd just be interested to see how the bastard reacted if I walked in. I bet he'd—"

But the girl called Chippy was cut short by another hissing voice, male this time, as a Floor Manager, complete with headphones, came up and asked what the hell was going on and what the hell they thought they were doing bursting into a studio while there was a rehearsal in progress and whether they would piss off out again double-quick or whether he'd have to bloody kick them out.

Sydnee peered out into the corridor as they beat their hasty retreat from Studio B, but all seemed to be clear. "We'd better go back on to our set," she said, and then, with a note almost of desperation in her voice, went on, "Barrett may be there, or John, or Jim. Then we can get your bit of rehearsal sorted out. Or the hats sorted out. Or something . . ."

She got them to wait in the corridor while she slipped to check that Studio A was clear of contestants and celebrities. She took her duties seriously.

Within a minute they were ushered back on to the red, blue and silver set. Sylvian the Mohican was still fiddling, unhappy with the alignment of the lectern in the centre of the floor. Three cameramen were slumped lethargically over their cameras. There were more people around than there had been earlier in the afternoon.

One of them was Jim Trace-Smith, the Producer. Since there was no sign of Barrett Doran, and the Executive Producer, John Mantle, had yet to return from his, er, important meeting, it had fallen to Jim Trace-Smith to brief the "professions" as to what they had to do.

The Producer was tall with dark-brown hair which stuck

out on his crown as if cut by a school barber. There was something boyish about his whole appearance. Even his pale-blue flying-suit looked as if it had come from Mother-care. His face would have been astonishingly youthful, but for the almost comical creases of anxiety which were etched in between the eyebrows. He had the air of someone who took life *very seriously indeed*.

Nor was this impression dispelled when he began to speak. His voice had a slight Midlands flatness which, even when his words expressed great enthusiasm, seemed impervious to animation.

"Good afternoon, one and all." He made what was perhaps intended to be an expansive gesture. "And may I say how delighted I am that you have agreed to join us in the fun of *Hats Off!*"

"*If The Cap Fits*," murmured Sydnee.

"Oh yes, *If The Cap Fits*. It's a really terrific game and I think there's no question that you're all going to have a ball. Now, as you've probably gathered, the show that we're recording tonight is what we call a 'pilot'. That means that we've all got to be our brilliant best, because, according to how we do this show, the 'powers-that-be' will decide whether or not they're going to make a series of this terrific game. And we all want to make sure that there is a series of *If The Cap Fits*—don't we?"

This proposal was heartily endorsed by three of the "professions". Charles thought he'd reserve judgement until he'd found out what the game involved.

"Does it mean," asked the one female in the party, "being a pilot, that what we record will actually go out on the box?"

"Oh, almost certainly, yes," the Producer lied. "As I say, it's a terrific game. I'm sure we've got the casting right, and I'm sure that what we record tonight will be the first show in a series that will run and run!"

He made this rallying-cry with all the bravura of a librarian turning down the central heating.

"Now I hope you're all beginning to understand what you'll have to do. You are involved only in Round One of our terrific game, but I'm sure you're going to get the show off to a great start. Now you've all been carefully selected by our highly-trained research team. . . ." He winked with awkward flirtatiousness at Sydnee, who ignored him. ". . . because you all represent some kind of profession. This profession will in each case be symbolized by a hat, but, just to confuse the contestants, you'll all be wearing the wrong hats. They have to guess who are the rightful owners of the various forms of headgear."

He then proceeded to explain that this was the reason for the game's name, a point which by now had penetrated the skull of even the dullest of the four "professions".

"Well," Jim Trace-Smith continued with limp heartiness, "have you all got your hats sorted out?"

"Erm, I'm afraid we're having a bit of a problem with Wardrobe about the hats . . ." Sydnee drew him to one side and a whispered discussion ensued.

When the Producer turned back to his audience, the furrows on his forehead were longer. "Well now, just got to actually sort out the hats, but can I just check what your professions are . . . ?"

He drew a list out of his flying-suit pocket. Charles had been one hundred per cent wrong. There was no bank cashier, no professional footballer and no dental nurse. Instead, his colleagues proved to be a hamburger chef, a surgeon and a stockbroker. Incredibly, the one female in the party turned out to be the stockbroker.

"We've got the actor's hat sorted out," Sydnee whispered, "but I don't know where Wardrobe have gone now, so I'm not sure about the others."

"I'll go and have a word with them," said Jim Trace-

Smith. "Now we'll need a tall white chef's hat for the chef. . . ."

"Actually that's not what I wear," the chef objected. "I have this little paper cap which—"

"So far as the public's concerned," Jim Trace-Smith overruled, "chefs wear tall white hats. Now for the surgeon we need one of those green mob-cap things. . . ."

"Actually I very rarely wear one of those. I . . ." But the surgeon thought better of it and stopped.

"Now we've got the actor's hat sorted out . . ."

"Well—" was as far as Charles was allowed to get.

"And for the stockbroker, obviously, a bowler hat."

"But I never wear a bowler hat."

"*So far as the public is concerned*, stockbrokers wear bowler hats!"

"But I'm a woman, for God's sake! You can't expect me to—"

How this argument would have resolved itself can only be matter for speculation, because at that moment Sydnee's restless eye caught sight of a man and a woman entering the far side of the studio. "Oh, my God, it's Bob Garston and Fiona Wakeford! Jim, the celebs are arriving! Quick, you lot, follow me!"

She started off, with her obedient foursome in tow, towards the exit that led to Studio B, but was stopped short in her tracks by the entry from it of a familiar bulky figure, followed by a dainty little woman in a fur coat and a short, balding, pale man.

"Oh God, it's Nick again! And Joanie Bruton! Quick! This way!"

The hamburger chef, the surgeon, the stockbroker and the actor, now as obsessed as their guardian with keeping their identities secret, dived after her through the door that led to the Control Gallery of Studio A, and left the set to the celebrities who were to be the stars of *If The Cap Fits*.

Chapter Two

JOHN MANTLE, EXECUTIVE Producer of *If The Cap Fits*, reckoned that he was doing well. As the third round of Armagnacs was served in Langan's Brasserie, he sneaked a covert look at his watch. Nearly half-past three. Even if they left within a quarter of an hour and got a taxi straight away, it would be well after four before they got back to W.E.T. House. And the longer they kept out of Studio A that afternoon, the better.

This thought was not prompted by laziness or an unwillingness to face his responsibilities. John Mantle was a deeply conscientious producer. He had been conscientious during the eight years he had spent learning his craft in the Light Entertainment Department of B.B.C. Television, and equally conscientious since, three years previously, he had moved to West End Television to do the same job for three times the money. But producing, he knew, did not only involve monitoring what went on in studios. That could frequently be left to an obedient underling, and he had the most biddable of lieutenants in Jim Trace-Smith, also from the B.B.C., whose invaluable attributes of diligence, even temper and total lack of imagination, John Mantle had quickly recognized, made him an ideal producer of Light Entertainment. The young man had been easily seduced into commercial television, again by the simple device of tripling his salary, thus becoming the first recruit to the entertainment empire John Mantle was slowly but surely annexing from his former employers.

The presence of Jim Trace-Smith in Studio A that afternoon at least ensured that the preparations for the pilot were proceeding, and freed the Executive Producer for more important duties, which in this case involved keeping his lunch guests out of Studio A as long as possible. The explosion when they finally got there was inevitable, but the later that happened, the less chance there would be of implementing the changes they were bound to demand.

There were two of them—Aaron Greenberg, podgy, grizzle-bearded, voluble, an untidy eater and drinker who allowed no word to go unsupported by an expansive gesture of his short arms; and Dirk van Henke, tall, blond, silent, drinking only Perrier water and constantly dabbing at his mouth with a corner of his table napkin. They represented the American copyright-holders of *Hats Off!*, the game show which had been successfully networked for three years in the States and the rights to whose format West End Television had bought for an almost unbelievable amount of money. They had followed the piloting and development of the show in the States and were thus the honoured bearers of the "Bible", that partly written but mostly unwritten stock of information and advice which would save any new developer of the show from falling into the format's most obvious pitfalls. They were extremely protective of their property, regarding any proposed change in the show as a direct personal assault.

Since their arrival in London two days previously, John Mantle had spent every waking hour justifying to Greenberg and van Henke the inevitable alterations which transatlantic relocation of the show demanded. They had fought everything; he had had to explain and re-explain each tiny kink and quibble of the revised format; but, by sheer, relentless, debilitating tact and the granting of a few minor concessions, the Executive Producer had managed to satisfy them that their baby, the property that, as Greenberg kept asserting, meant "somebody's gonna make a pot", was being treated with the care and respect that was its due. They now knew about every change and, grudgingly, they had accepted them all.

Except the title.

John Mantle had first broached the subject in the hire-car back from Heathrow, where he had personally met their Concorde flight. He had explained that *Hats Off!* did not have the right sound for a British game show, and that, after careful assessment of many possible alternatives, West End Television had decided on *If The Cap Fits*.

"What the shit does that mean?" Aaron Greenberg had asked.

"Well, it's a kind of saying. A proverb, if you like. 'If the cap fits, put it on.' It means, if something applies to you, then it applies to you . . ." John Mantle had continued feebly. "It's a very common expression. Very right for the show. Don't you have that proverb in the States?"

Aaron Greenberg snorted. "I never heard of it."

"I think," said Dirk van Henke in his quiet, precise voice, "our equivalent would be: 'If the shoe fits, wear it.'"

"Yes. That sounds as if it has the same meaning." John Mantle smiled enthusiastically at this point of contact.

"Shit," objected Aaron Greenberg. "You're not suggest-ing we call the show *If The Shoe Fits*? I mean, hell, it's about hats, not shoes."

"Yes, I know that. Of course I'm not suggesting we call it *If The Shoe Fits*."

"Thank Christ for that. Otherwise you would have screwed yourself out of a deal that's gonna make a pot for somebody."

"No, I'm suggesting we call it *If The Cap Fits*."

"No way. Forget it."

"But—"

"*Hats Off!*" Dirk van Henke insisted softly. "*Hats Off!*

23

That is the name of the show. Call it anything else and we don't have a deal."

The Executive Producer had left it there for the time being. Much of his work consisted of confronting people with unpalatable facts, and he knew that the most important element in any such presentation was always its timing. After he had deposited his guests at the Savoy, where they were going to "shower and sleep off the Concorde-lag", he had returned to W.E.T. House and got on to the Legal Department, who had negotiated the long, wrangling purchase of the rights to develop the *Hats Off!* format. He wanted to know where he stood legally on changing the title.

Like everything to do with the law, the situation turned out to be ambiguous. The relevant clause was:

> *The licensees agree not to adapt, rearrange or alter the format in any way without the approval of the owner, such approval not to be unreasonably withheld.*

The crux of the issue was, of course, the last phrase, in particular its penultimate word. What was unreasonable? This, as the Legal Department advised him unhelpfully, was a matter of interpretation. They would investigate and get back to him.

The Executive Producer assessed the position. The set had been designed and built with the changed title all over it. The music links had been recorded. Even if there had been time to reverse the decision, alterations at this late stage would represent considerable expense. And John Mantle always prided himself on keeping within his budgets.

He decided to sit it out. He'd wait and hear what the Legal Department advised when they came back to him, but, unless that was really bad, he would stick by his original decision. It would inevitably lead to tantrums from

Greenberg and van Henke, but, if they only found out about the new title on the afternoon of the recording, he judged they would have little opportunity to do anything about it. And, once the show had gone down well in front of the audience, he felt confident that they would be less worried about the change.

He kept his nerve pretty well for the next couple of days. Once he almost lost it, and that moment of uncertainty had led to the confusion of the title at Reception which Charles Paris had encountered. But basically the Executive Producer reckoned he'd get away with it. The Legal Department, when they finally came back to him, had little to add. Everything still depended on the interpretation of the word "unreasonably", and they couldn't really say how that decision would go in a court of law unless the issue actually *went* to a court of law. In other words, the lawyers proved as helpful as ever.

John Mantle offered more drinks, but even Aaron Greenberg refused this time. As he settled the bill with his American Express Gold Card, the Executive Producer stole another look at his watch. Nearly four. The show started recording at seven-thirty. Only a few hours to survive the Americans' wrath.

On the way out of the Brasserie, he greeted West End Television's Head of Drama who was coming to the end of lunch with a moderately famous actress. As a further delaying tactic, he introduced the couple to his guests. Since the actress had recently been seen in a *Masterpiece Theatre* in the States, conversation developed satisfactorily.

John Mantle was discussing a vicious point of W.E.T. politics with his colleague, when he overheard Greenberg saying, "Yeah, and do you know what they wanted to call it? Only *If The Cap Fits!*"

"Really?" The moderately famous actress chuckled throatily. "Why—is it a show about contraception?"

Aaron Greenberg looked puzzled. "What's that supposed to mean?"

"Cap, darling. Cap. Dutch cap. A form of female contraception."

The American shook his shaggy head, still bewildered.

"It's a thing you put . . ." The moderately famous actress gave another throaty chuckle. "I'm afraid we're liable to get a bit technical here. It's a . . . what would you call it? A diaphragm!"

"A diaphragm?" Aaron Greenberg echoed. "You hear that, Dirk? You know that dumb title they wanted to use? *If The Cap Fits*. You know what a 'cap' means over here? A diaphragm! A diaphragm, for Christ's sakes!"

John Mantle ushered his guests grimly out of the restaurant. He was not looking forward to the next couple of hours.

Sydnee's game of hide-and-seek with the hamburger chef, the surgeon, the stockbroker and the actor had continued through the afternoon. They had finally had their inappropriate hats grudgingly fitted in Wardrobe, been shown where to stand on the red, blue and silver set, and been conducted up five floors of W.E.T. House to the Conference Room where they were to await their call. Unfortunately, when Sydnee opened the door, she found the four noncelebrity contestants who were to play *If The Cap Fits* already ensconced, and had to beat another hasty retreat.

She led her four charges into an empty office, found a phone and immediately punched four digits. "Hello. Mandy? Listen, how many Conference Rooms got booked for this pilot today? Well, no, there should have been three. Yes, I know on *Funny Money* it's one for the celebs and one for the punt- . . . for the members of the public, but in this game we've got two different sets of members of the public and they mustn't meet. Yes, well . . . what? No, we couldn't put the contestants in with them. Mixing with members of the public? . . . the celebs'd never wear it. No. Well, is there another Conference Room free? Oh, shit. No, no, okay, not your fault. Don't worry. I'll sort something out. Yes, after this little holocaust, fine. 'Bye."

She turned to face the hamburger chef, the surgeon, the stockbroker and the actor. "Sorry. Cock-up on booking. I'm afraid you're going to have to wait here in the Production Office." She gestured round the room. "Welcome to where I work. I'll organize some drinks and things for you later."

"What's that?" The one female in the party pointed up at a wall which was covered with small head-and-shoulders snapshots pinned up in rows.

"Oh, that's our 'Ugly Wall'," Sydnee replied. Then she seemed to wish she hadn't said it and try to cover up. "I mean, it's a very ugly wall, so we just try to stick as many things as possible on it."

The stockbroker looked more closely at the snapshots. "These look like the sort of pictures we had to send in when we got your form about taking part in game shows."

"Oh, do they?" asked Sydnee innocently. "Now, can I get you all a tea or coffee? I'm afraid you're going to have rather a long wait. You must understand, with a pilot it's always a bit difficult to work out quite how long all the rehearsal's going to take. I'm sure we'd get it sorted out better if the show ever went to a series."

"I thought," the stockbroker objected, "the producer said it definitely would go to a series."

"Oh yes. Yes, of course," said Sydnee.

The office door opened and a tall man with steel-grey hair and thickly-lashed blue eyes entered. Ignoring the other four, he walked straight up to Sydnee. "Where the bloody hell have you been? Have you got that list of 'hat' lines?" he demanded brusquely.

"Oh yes." She reached into a drawer and produced a few

typewritten sheets. "I went through all the dictionaries and books of quotations. I should think you ought to be able to work out some links from that lot."

"I'll see. Other thing, check my glass on the set after rehearsal."

"Your glass?"

"Its contents."

"Oh. Oh yes," said Sydnee, understanding.

The four "professions" remained mystified by this exchange, but the stockbroker, bolder than the others, addressed the grey-haired man. "It's Barrett Doran, isn't it?"

He turned on her the kind of look rose-growers reserve for greenfly. "What?"

Sydnee stepped into the breach. "Barrett, these four are the 'professions' for the First Round."

"Oh," said Barrett Doran without interest, and turned to leave the room. But, as he reached it, the door opened and he was confronted by a pale youth with ginger hair and an apologetic expression.

"Ah, Barrett. I was looking for you. I have worked out a few one-liners on the 'hat' theme. If you want to cast your eye over them, I'll be happy to—"

"I do my own links," said Barrett Doran. "I don't need any of your bloody crap." And he walked out of the office.

The pale youth let the door close behind him and looked at the five who stood there. His face was vulnerable, almost tearful. "Hello, Sydnee. If there's anything I can . . . you know, for this lot. . . ."

She introduced him to the hamburger chef, the surgeon, the stockbroker and the actor. "Jeremy Fowler's our Script Associate on the show. He's got an endless supply of funny lines for all the contestants and everyone. You know, so if you want to have a few witty ripostes, and you can't think of any yourself, ask Jeremy."

The youth smiled weakly. "I have got a few lines. I mean, I

28

only got the list of your professions late yesterday, but I have worked out a few things you might say."

"When?" asked the hamburger chef.

"When?"

"When might we want to say them?"

"Oh. Well, for example, when you've got the wrong hat on. I mean, say someone puts the surgeon's hat on you and you're asked if you are a surgeon, you could say, 'I don't think I'd be cut out for the job.'"

"Why?"

"What do you mean—why?"

"Well, why should I say that?"

"It's a joke."

"Is it?"

"Well, a sort of joke. Not a marvellous one, I agree," Jeremy Fowler conceded, "but it's the sort of thing that might get a laugh if you pong it enough."

"*Pong* it?"

"Yes."

"I don't understand it."

"Well, it's a sort of pun. 'Cut out for the job' . . . surgeon . . . *cut* out. . . .'"

"Oh," said the hamburger chef seriously. "Oh, I see. I don't think I probably will say that, actually."

"Ah, well. Never mind. I've got a few lines for the rest of you . . . you know, if you think you might need them. . . . They will get an opportunity to say something, won't they, Sydnee?"

"A bit, I should think. It really depends how Barrett plays it."

"Yes. Well, as I say, I have got a few lines about, you know, being a hamburger chef . . . or a stockbroker . . . or an actor . . . or not being them. . . . You know, these games always sound better if you get a bit of repartee going with the host . . . I mean. . . . Anyone fancy any lines . . . ? I could write them down on cards for you or. . . . Well, if you do want any, you only have to ask . . . as I say. . . . It's up to you, really. . ."

He ran aground on silence.

"Right," asked Sydnee brightly. "How many teas, how many coffees?"

There was a marked contrast in moods in the two Conference Rooms that had been properly booked. One contained the four contestants who were actually going to play *If The Cap Fits*, the other the celebrities whose role was to add a little glamour to the show. In the first there was an atmosphere of obsessive nervousness; in the second, of equally obsessive insouciance.

For the four contestants, the day was the culmination of a long process. They had all originally written in to West End Television, saying how suitable they thought they would be as contestants in the company's major, long-running give-away show, *Funny Money*. In reply to their letters they had been sent a yellow questionnaire, asking information about age, marital status, work, hobbies and "any amusing incidents that may have happened in your life". They had been requested to return the completed form, together with a recent photograph. It was these snapshots which ruled out most of the candidates. Television game shows are constructed on the premise that everyone is attractive, and those whose looks did not meet the researchers' approval had their participation in the world of television restricted to an appearance on Sydnee's "Ugly Wall".

Those who survived the scrutiny were requested to appear for interview at a large hotel in their locality on a given date. This date was not negotiable; those who couldn't make it lost their chances of participating in the show. At the interview (which for most of the candidates involved taking a day off work) they were chatted to for up to an hour by Sydnee or another of the researchers, who then decided which contenders attained that level of cheery triviality which game shows demanded.

The four in the Conference Room, having overcome all these hurdles, had been not a little disappointed when their magic phone-calls finally came through. Yes, they had been very impressive in their interviews. They were just the sort of people who would be ideal game show contestants. Unfortunately, W.E.T. had got all the participants required for the current series of *Funny Money*. But the company was about to launch a new game show, bound to be quite as successful as the other—would they like to be in on the start of a milestone in television history?

This was not what most of them had had in mind, but they all (in one case only after checking the value of the prizes that were to be given away) agreed to participate. The initial call had been followed by a letter, outlining the format of *If The Cap Fits*, and then further phone-calls making detailed arrangements about transport and, where necessary, overnight accommodation.

And there they were, actually in a Conference Room in W.E.T. House, guarded by one of Sydnee's fellow-researchers (with the equally silly name of Chita), and about to go down to Studio A to run through the game with the host, the notoriously good-looking and popular Barrett Doran. It was enough to make anyone a bit nervous.

But their nervousness took different forms, because for each of them the prospect of appearing on television had a different significance. For Trish Osborne, who, though she bitterly resented the description, would be introduced on the show as "a housewife from Billericay", it was a symbolic act, a new start to her fifth decade, a decade in which she intended to assert her own individuality, to be herself rather than somebody's wife or somebody's mother. She had a momentary doubt, wondering whether the silk blouse and skimpy brassière eventually selected for her appearance in front of the cameras was quite suitable, but she bit it back. This was her, Trish Osborne. She was going to prove that she had as much to offer as all those professional television people. She was going to make an impression. This was going to be the start of something.

For Tim Dyer, participating in *If The Cap Fits* signified something else entirely. For him it was a chance to win, and he was determined that that was what he was going to do. He had studied many game shows from his armchair, making notes on the techniques used by successful contestants. He had spent a long time checking through the format of the new game, and had boned up on General Knowledge and recent international news. He, needless to say, had been the one who had asked about the value of the prizes, and he felt confident that he could finish the evening at least £800 richer, with a video-recorder and camera, the prospect of a champagne weekend for two in Amsterdam and, if all went well, as the owner of a brand-new Austin Metro.

He had prepared himself as far as he could; now all he needed was a little luck. And that luck hinged mainly on which celebrity he was paired with. Joanie Bruton he reckoned was the most intelligent, though Bob Garston was also pretty bright. Either of them would do. Just so long as he didn't get lined up with that thick boxer, Nick Jeffries. Or even worse that dumb actress, Fiona Wakeford. Tim Dyer sat in the Conference Room, praying to that very specialized deity, the God of Game Shows.

In the other Conference Room the objects of his speculation lounged around, studiously laid-back.

None admitted to having read the format of *If The Cap Fits*, which had been sent to them, because this had overtones of swotting, taking the show more seriously than was fitting for someone of celebrity status. Nor had they shown much apparent interest when, first the researcher who was in charge of them, and then Jim Trace-Smith himself, had taken them through the mechanics of the game. It didn't do to look as if it mattered. There were two acceptable attitudes for the celebrities. The first was bonhomous condescension, as if one were helping West End Television out of a spot by taking part, just because one was that sort of person. The second was mercenary bewilderment . . . "The agent rang about it, I said how much, he said three hundred quid . . . well, I thought, I was only going to watch the box tonight otherwise, so what the hell, why not do it?"

They were a contrasted quartet, who might have prompted a philosophical observer to speculate on the nature of celebrity. However, the only observer present was a researcher called Quentin, so armoured with cynicism and so unsurprised by anything that television or fame could bombard him with, that such philosophical speculations did not arise.

Nick Jeffries' boxing career had ended three years previously. Its start, his winning of an Olympic bronze medal in the Middleweight division, had prompted the customary excesses of the British sporting press, who promised him a professional career of pure gold and saluted a future World Champion. He had held domestic and European titles for a while, but, when projected on to the world stage, had been so comprehensively defeated by the Number Eight contender that his boxing career virtually ended with that fight. However, his face was familiar to the British public through his many endorsements of sportswear, and since, unlike many in his chosen profession, he was capable of speech, he was taken up by a shrewd personal management and marketed as a celebrity. His long-term aim (which he would not achieve) was to attain that level of lovability which the British public had accorded to Henry Cooper. His short-term aim that afternoon (which would be achieved much more easily) was to chat up Fiona Wakeford.

She was an actress who had risen to public notice in a popular W.E.T. sit. com., *Who's Your Friend?*, in which she played a pretty but totally brainless actress. Since this did not involve the slightest effort of acting on her part, her career looked set fair to be very successful. She didn't mind Nick Jeffries chatting her up. In fact, she was so used to everyone chatting her up that she was hardly aware of it. She wasn't aware of much, actually.

The other woman panellist was a very different proposition. Joanie Bruton had started life as a journalist on local newspapers and then moved towards women's magazines. The illness of the regular contributor on one of these had forced her one week to write the agony column, and she discovered such an aptitude for this line of work that within three years she had become a nationally-recognized guru, whose advice was solicited and respected on every embarrassing topic. Her petite good looks, forthright manner and boundless energy had quickly established her as a popular television personality. She made no secret of her appetite for hard work, and, when interviewed (which she was quite frequently) constantly paid tribute to the support of her husband, Roger, who had given up his own Civil Service job in the Department of Health and Social Security to manage the business side of her burgeoning career. He was there in the Conference Room that afternoon, a pale, rather breathlessly fat figure, checking through a pile of correspondence with his untiring spouse.

The fourth celebrity also appeared to be working, though the restlessness in his eyes suggested that he was motivated more by keeping up with the Joneses (or, in this case, the Brutons) than from a genuine desire to read the television script in front of him (which of course had nothing to do with *If The Cap Fits*; it was for a B.B.C. series called *Joe Soap*).

Bob Garston was a television journalist of the "New Hearty" school. He had risen through those programmes of the late Seventies which had taken up serious causes like consumerism and treated them with such unremitting facetiousness that they produced a television equivalent of the tabloid press. He was the sort of presenter for whom no word was allowed out unsupported by a picture and no opinion unsupported by a pun. He worked assiduously on his image as a man of the people, and prided himself on the fact that the audience identified with him. In his heart of hearts he felt superior to everyone, but that afternoon, as he neglectfully scanned the script in front of him, he looked disgruntled.

The door to the Conference Room opened. Quentin, the guardian researcher, glanced up protectively, but then relaxed as Jeremy Fowler sidled in with his customary air of apology.

"Er, good afternoon. I'm the Script Associate on this show. . . . I've worked out a few lines, you know, that some of you might want to use . . ."

"What sort of lines?" asked Joanie Bruton.

"Well, you know, er, funny lines . . . I mean, there may be a moment when you want to make a joke and, er, well, I've worked out a few jokes that might be suitable . . ."

"Oh, I'm hopeless when I try to do that," confessed Fiona Wakeford. "Honestly, I can never remember the line, and I get the joke all wrong and it's worse than if I hadn't said anything. I'm terribly stupid."

No one contradicted her. Joanie Bruton and Bob Garston returned to their work, but Nick Jeffries looked interested. He recognized his limitations in the field of repartee. "What sort of lines you got?"

"Well, erm, a lot of hat jokes. I mean, the show being about hats . . . you know . . ."

"Like . . . ?"

"Well, erm, there's this one about the man whose neighbour's dog eats his hat. . . ."

"Who—the neighbour's hat?"

"No, no, the man's hat. And the man goes to complain, and the neighbour gets belligerent . . ."

"Gets what?"

"Gets angry. . . . And the man says, 'I don't like your attitude', and the neighbour says, 'It wasn't *my* attitude, it was *your* attitude!'"

"Eh?"

"It's a pun. Attitude. 'At . . . 'e . . . chewed. Hat. You see, the dog had chewed the hat. Get it?"

"Not really. I mean, this bloke didn't like the other bloke's attitude, I get that. But what I don't see is . . ."

The explanation of the joke might have gone on for some time, had the door not opened at that moment to admit John Mantle, still with his two Americans in tow. He was still playing his delaying game and keeping them out of Studio A. The detour up to the Fifth Floor Conference Room, ostensibly just to introduce the copyright-holders to the panellists, was, he reckoned, worth at least ten minutes. But he knew he couldn't keep them in ignorance much longer.

While introductions were taking place, the telephone rang and was answered by the researcher. "All wanted down in studio," he announced, "to meet the contestants."

"Oh Jesus! I didn't think we'd have to see that lot till the actual recording," complained Bob Garston, the man of the people.

"Sorry. We've got to just run through a bit of rehearsal on the bits you do with them."

"Shit," said Bob Garston, with bad grace.

John Mantle decided that they'd all go down to Studio A together. He knew that he could no longer put off the crisis, but he hoped his American guests' reactions might be a little inhibited by the presence of the celebrities.

It was a vain hope. The minute the party walked on to the set, Aaron Greenberg looked up at the red wheel with its silver lettering and screamed, "Christ Almighty! What the shit is that supposed to be?"

"John," Dirk van Henke hissed in the Executive Producer's ear, "you have just lost the rights in *Hats Off!*"

Chapter Three

JOHN MANTLE WAS no fool. He had been prepared for this reaction, and he had planned how to deal with it. For the time being, he led the two furious Americans up to his office and let the wave of anger wash over him.

"I mean, for Christ's sakes!" Aaron Greenberg was spluttering. "What kind of a show do you think this is? We can't have that kind of talk on a show like this. Diaphragms? No way. I mean, this is meant to be wholesome family entertainment. This show will be going out to Middle America."

"Actually, it won't be. You forget that—"

"Okay, Middle Europe. Who's counting?"

"Not actually Europe. This is England and—"

"England—Europe—what's the difference? The point is that, wherever it is, there are gonna be little old ladies out there who know what they want and who aren't gonna to want to turn on a show about diaphragms."

"That isn't the first meaning most people will think of when they hear the title."

"No? Well, listen, smartass, I've only mentioned it to one person and that's what she thought."

"I'm not sure that actresses are typical of—"

"Don't you try telling me what's typical or not typical! All I know is that you're calling this show by the wrong name! And that's going to lose you your audience and lose you the chance of making a pot. I mean, for Christ's sakes, we're talking about the Golden Goose here and you're

38

trying to wring its neck before it's laid a single goddamned egg!"

"What is more," Dirk van Henke insinuated, "you are in breach of contract."

John Mantle let them go on. In a little while, he would summon his adviser from the Legal Department. Then maybe the Americans would produce a London-based lawyer to fight their side. All that would take time and, even if eventually they could take out some sort of injunction to stop W.E.T. from proceeding with the show (which, on balance, John Mantle thought was unlikely), there was a strong chance that by then the pilot would be recorded.

So he rode out the storm, confident all the while that downstairs in Studio A rehearsals for *If The Cap Fits* were still going on.

Barrett Doran was no keener to meet the contestants than Bob Garston had been, but Jim Trace-Smith insisted that they must rehearse the basic sequence of the show or the whole thing would be a shambles when they came to record it. Barrett Doran grudgingly agreed to this, though he was not going to put himself out by being polite to anybody.

His first action, on coming into the studio, was to look at the red, blue and silver set in horror. "Jesus," he said, "what the hell's this? I didn't know the show was meant to be set in a bloody fast food restaurant. Is it no longer possible to get professional designers? What's the problem—money? Is that why we have to put up with this crap?"

Sylvian de Beaune, who had been slumped in the front row of the audience seating, rose as if to protest, but thought better of it, turned on his heel and flounced out of the studio. Jim Trace-Smith's eyes followed him out, then realized that the rehearsal must be moved along to cover this awkwardness.

"Now, for the First Round," he said, with his customary

limp élan, "each of the contestants has to be paired up with one of the celebrities. This is where they have to change round the hats on the four 'professions', and they're allowed to consult on this."

"Seems to make it unnecessarily complicated."

"I'm afraid that's how the format works, Barrett. Anyway, the viewing audience likes it. We've done some research on this and we've found out that people at home enjoy seeing the contestants and celebrities being all pals together."

"Do they really?" growled the lovable Barrett Doran. "All right, you lot!" He gestured imperiously to the four contestants. "Come over here. Each of you's got to pair up with one of the panel for the First Round." He turned to where the four celebrities sat at their long blue desk, sipping from their red-and-blue-striped glasses and discussing their tax problems. "Now we'll do it so's we get a man and a woman in each line-up, so you, lady, go with Bob, you with Nick, you with Joanie and you with Fiona. Got that?"

"Erm," Tim Dyer objected. "Can we change it round? I'd rather be paired with Joanie."

"Would you?" snapped Barrett Doran. "Well, I don't give a wet fart what you'd rather do. The pairings will be as I said."

Tim Dyer wasn't going to stand for that. He'd just been round the back of the set and seen the gleaming, brand-new Metro waiting for the moment when it would be driven on to awestruck "Aaah"s from the studio audience. "But I don't want to be with Fiona," he insisted.

"Why, isn't she pretty enough for you? You think yourself damned lucky. It's the nearest a little shit like you's ever going to get to a bit of crumpet like that." The host turned to his producer. "What do you want them to do—stand behind the panellist they're paired with?"

"Yes, behind, slightly to the right. Then we can get them in a nice close two-shot."

"Okay. Get to those positions." Barrett Doran looked petulantly back at Jim Trace-Smith. "Do you really want us to go right through the whole bloody thing?"

"We have to make sure everyone knows what they've got to do, where they've got to stand, that kind of number. . . ."

"Okay, okay." Barrett Doran went across to his lectern and stood there, drumming his fingers on its top.

Various researchers and Stage Managers were recruited to stand in the positions later to be occupied by the hamburger chef, the surgeon, the stockbroker and the actor. Some unrepresentative hats had been procured for them (though not from Wardrobe, who said they were still not convinced that they should be providing hats for the actual recording, but were damned sure they weren't going to provide any for rehearsal). The researchers and Stage Managers then invented professions for themselves and the contestants, with celebrity help, tried to say who should be wearing which hat. Since the hats were wrong anyway, all this took a long time. Barrett Doran conducted the proceedings without even a pretence of geniality.

At the end of the round, Jim Trace-Smith reminded the contestants that they would be awarded money prizes at this point, but that the one with least points would be eliminated. Tim Dyer objected volubly that he would be working under an unfair handicap because Fiona Wakeford was so stupid. The actress proved not quite stupid enough not to realize that this was an insult, and burst out crying. Nick Jeffries threatened to punch Tim Dyer's teeth out through his arse. Jim Trace-Smith managed to reimpose a kind of calm.

In the next round each of the celebrities was supplied with a hat-box by "the lovely Nikki and the lovely Linzi", two terminally bored-looking models who were part of the set-decoration. The remaining three contestants were then given the names of four types of hat and had in turn to guess whose hat-box contained which hat, helped or misled by clues from the celebrities.

Trish Osborne was the first to play in this round. She had found that, once on the set, her nerves had given way to a mood of almost manic confidence. It was going to be all right. She would manage. Better than that, she would do very well. She would really make an impression.

As she stood beside Barrett Doran at the lectern, he flashed her a big smile. Looking at her for the first time, he had realized that she was rather attractive and thought it might be worth beaming a little of his charm in her direction. Nice short dark hair, full lips, nice trim little figure. Maybe he might invite her to his dressing room for a drink before the recording. . . . He gave her the practice list of four hats— fedora, fire-helmet, beret and baseball cap. Trish started chatting with the celebrities, moving round to her decision. She felt in control. She was doing well.

"Oh God!" Barrett Doran suddenly exclaimed.

Trish Osborne turned curiously towards him.

"Look at her. We can't have this. I mean, God, this is peak viewing, a family show. We can't have her looking like that."

Trish unwillingly followed the line of his accusing finger, which pointed straight at her bust. In the excitement of the occasion, she saw that both of her nipples had hardened, a fact which the thin blouse and brassière did nothing to disguise.

Jim Trace-Smith came forward, nonplussed. It was not a situation he had had to deal with before, and he wasn't quite sure of the correct procedure.

"Well, come on," shouted Barrett Doran. "Do something. Get her off to Wardrobe. We can't have her looking as if she's panting for it like that. This isn't a bloody tit show, is it?"

At this point, Trish Osborne, utterly deserted by her new confidence, started to cry. She was led off with meaningless words of comfort by the researcher, Chita. In Wardrobe, after an unsuccessful experiment with Sellotape, her nipples were contained by two sticking plasters.

The rehearsal had to stop at six, so that everyone involved in Studio A could get their statutory hour's meal-break and the cameras could be lined up, before the audience was admitted at seven, ready for the seven-thirty recording. When the rehearsal ended, the celebrities and contestants had a variety of options as to where they could go. They could eat in the canteen, they could go and titivate, prepare or relax in their dressing rooms, or they could return to their separate Conference Rooms, now converted by the introduction of alcohol into Hospitality Rooms.

For the hamburger chef, the surgeon, the stockbroker and the actor, who had been stuck in the Production Office all afternoon, there were less options. Sydnee, still desperate to keep them apart from the other participants in *If The Cap Fits*, had ruled out their visiting the canteen, and arranged for sandwiches to be brought up to the office. There was, of course, no question of their sharing the largesse of Hospitality in the two Conference Rooms, but, after considerable thought and a few exploratory phone-calls, she decided that it might be safe for them to go downstairs to the W.E.T. bar, "if any of them wanted to".

Charles Paris was the first to state that he did want to. It had been a boring afternoon, it promised to be a boring evening, and he had long since discovered the beneficial properties of alcohol in the treatment of boredom. Since his only responsibilities in the show were standing up and putting on different hats, he did not have any anxiety about drink blunting his performing edge. He just knew that he would feel considerably more human with two or three large Bell's inside him.

Sydnee led the four of them conspiratorially down the

43

back-stairs to the bar, which was very crowded. As well as the flood of after-work drinkers from the offices above, there were also many of the Studio A technicians and a lot of the team from Studio B, whose recording schedule for *Method In Their Murders* incorporated the same meal-break.

"I'll dive in and get you some drinks," said Sydnee bravely. "Then I must sort out your Make-up calls. That's going to be the most difficult bit of all. There's only one Make-up room and we've got to ensure that you don't meet any of the others in there. Anyway, what will you all drink?"

She took their orders, and thrust her way into the mêlée round the bar. The four "professions" stood around awkwardly. There was nowhere to sit and the afternoon upstairs had long since exhausted their limited stock of mutual conversation.

Charles saw a little knot of people gathered round Melvyn Gasc, the presenter of *Method In Their Murders*. Gasc had risen to prominence in the previous few years as a pop scientist and, like most who do well on television in that role, was more valued for his eccentricity than his academic qualifications. His plumpness, his broken French accent and his windmilling gestures all made him a readily identifiable persona, which coincided easily with the general public's view of scientists as mad professors. They also made him popular fodder for television impressionists, and Charles thought he could detect an element of self-parody in the vigorous way Gasc was addressing his circle of sycophants.

One of this circle was the girl, Chippy, whom the "professions" had met on their hurried excursion into Studio B. In better lighting she proved to be strikingly pretty, with wispy blond hair and deep-set dark-blue eyes which gave her an air of melancholy, or even tragedy. As Charles watched, she detached herself from the group and moved towards the door, through which Barrett Doran had just entered.

But she had no opportunity to speak to the host of *If The*

Cap Fits. He was immediately swept up by an earnest-looking man in a suit, accompanied by a short, dark, bearded man and a tall, thin, blond one. They were close enough for Charles to hear their conversation.

"Barrett," said the man in the suit, who was John Mantle. "Aaron and Dirk were watching a bit of the rehearsal, and they've got a few points."

"Have they?" growled Barrett Doran. "Get me a large gin."

The Executive Producer, apparently cowed by the directness of this order (though in fact shrewdly deciding to leave his game-show host and copyright-holders alone to discuss their differences), made for the bar.

"Now what the hell is this?"

Aaron Greenberg looked Doran full in the eye. "Just that with you the show is dying."

"Oh yes?"

"Yes. You aren't getting anything out of these contestants. Okay, they're a bunch of loxes—God knows why your researchers couldn't come up with some with a bit more 'pazazz'—but it's still up to you to get a bit of life out of them. The show's coming across like a pile of old dog-shit, and that's because you're such a bummer. If you stay on as host, it's not going to work and the company's going to lose the chance of making a pot. I mean, Eddie, who fronts the show in the States, would never allow anyone to—"

"I don't give a shit what Eddie would or wouldn't allow. I am doing this show—got that? I know my public, I know what they want, and, come the recording, that is what I will give them. So just keep your big nose out of this—Okay? I've been in this business too long to take advice from some jumped-up little Yid!"

For a second it looked as if Greenberg would hit him, but Dirk van Henke laid a restraining hand on his associate's arm and it didn't happen. Barrett Doran turned away from them and met John Mantle returning from the bar with a large straight gin. He snatched it and hissed at the Executive Producer, "I'll be in my dressing room. Keep this shit off my back—all right? Or you find yourself another presenter."

He moved towards the exit, then caught sight of Sydnee, moving, laden with drinks, from the bar. "You sorted out that glass for me?" he demanded.

She nodded. "It's done."

As he made for the door, Chippy moved forward as if to speak to him. Barrett Doran looked right through her.

She recoiled, her face even more tragic, and came disconsolately over towards the group to whom Sydnee was dispensing drinks.

"Now, there we are . . . a pint, lager and lime, dry white wine, and . . . yours was the gin and tonic, Charles? Right?"

"Oh. I asked for a whisky, actually."

"Ah." Sydnee looked back hopelessly at the increasing crowd around the bar.

"Never mind. That's fine," said Charles, taking the drink, prepared to change the habits of a lifetime. He didn't like the taste of gin much, but alcohol was alcohol.

Chippy looked as if she wanted to speak to her friend, but she was interrupted by the arrival of a young man, whose earphones and transmitter identified him as a Floor Manager. "Chippy, Clayton wants to go and have something to eat. Can you go and cover in the studio while he's off?"

"I suppose so." Chippy didn't sound keen on the idea.

"He's waiting till you come."

"Okay." She turned to Sydnee. "Listen, we'll talk later. Okay?"

"Sure. What have you got to do?"

"Keep an eye on the props in Studio B. We've got some rather valuable—not to say dangerous—stuff down there."

"Sure. See you."

46

Chippy wandered sadly off, and Sydnee went to phone Make-up and try and sort out a schedule for getting the "professions" made up without meeting anyone they shouldn't. Make-up was proving to be a head-ache. Already the girls were having to work through their meal-break, which was going to put them on time-and-a-half. At least. Which was going to bump up the budget. Which would not please John Mantle.

The hamburger chef, the surgeon, the stockbroker and the actor stood, sipping their drinks, avoiding each other's eyes, unable to dredge up even the most fatuous scrap of conversation.

Charles Paris downed his gin and tonic, grimacing at the unfamiliar taste. He needed another drink. He hadn't bothered to bring a bottle with him, relying on television's usual plethora of Hospitality Rooms. But it looked as if on this occasion he might have come unstuck. He was going to have to stock up for the evening.

He didn't offer to buy drinks for the others. For one thing, none of them had finished their first round; for another, spending the whole afternoon with them had induced in Charles a kind of selfish misanthropy.

But his path to the bar was obstructed by Sydnee.

"I've sorted it out with Make-up. You're to go down first."

"When?"

"Now. Straight away."

"Oh, but I was just going to get another drink."

"Isn't time. Sorry. They're just finishing with Joanie Bruton at the moment. Then one of the contestants is going in at quarter to seven. They want you at half-past six. Can you go straight there?"

"Well, I—"

"Thanks. And can you be sure you go down the back-stairs, through Studio B and then through Studio A? That way there's no risk of you meeting anyone you shouldn't. You know where Make-up is when you come out of Studio A?"

Charles nodded, and left the bar with bad grace. He really needed another drink. It was bad enough to be given a gin instead of a whisky, but then to only have one. . . . It had only been a single, anyway. . . . He felt hard-done-by.

He stomped down the back-stairs, then into Studio B. There was no one about. The cameras were set facing their test-cards, ready for the half-hour's statutory line-up before the recording. The set looked unchanged, with its random scatterings of weapons and phials of chemicals. If Chippy was there guarding the exhibits from Melvyn Gasc's Black Museum, there was no sign of her.

He pushed through the double doors out of Studio B into the corridor, where he encountered the black-leather-clad designer, Sylvian de Beaune, who was pacing anxiously up and down.

"Set looks really terrific," said Charles encouragingly.

"I hope so." The designer did not seem to be convinced. "I hope so," he repeated, and walked off towards the lifts. Charles pushed through the double doors into Studio A, and found himself alone in the huge, dimly-lit space.

He was halfway across the set when he had the thought. Still feeling self-pityingly disgruntled about only having had one drink, he suddenly remembered Barrett Doran's words to Sydnee about his glass.

It was worth trying. With a look round to check that he was not observed, Charles went across to the blue, triangular lectern. On it stood a red-and-blue-striped carafe and a red-and-blue-striped glass. Both were full of colourless fluid.

The contents of the carafe had no smell.

But the contents of the glass smelt reassuringly of gin.

So that was how Barrett Doran fuelled his bonhomie in front of the cameras.

48

Charles looked at his watch. Nearly half-past six. He'd have to hurry to Make-up.

Still, that sod Barrett Doran could spare it.

Charles took a long swig from the glass.

Then, opting for a sheep-as-lamb philosophy, he took another.

The alcohol burned comfortingly inside him.

He topped up the glass with water from the carafe, and, feeling more cheerful, went out of the studio to Make-up.

Chapter Four

THE AUDIENCE WHO came to Studio A that evening had, to
some extent, been victims of the same disillusionment as the
contestants. All of them, applying either as individuals or
on behalf of such organizations as Townswomen's Guilds,
insurance company social clubs and amateur dramatic
societies, had written in asking for tickets to attend a recording of that very popular, long-established game show, *Funny
Money*. They had all, instead, been offered tickets for a
brand-new game show entitled (as far as they were concerned—indeed, as far as everyone except two irate Americans was concerned) *If The Cap Fits*. There had been few
rejections of the offer. After all, television was television, and
the show didn't really matter so much as the fact of actually
being there.

For many of them, it was their first visit to a television
studio, and they gazed around with fascination at the sus-
pended monitors above their heads and the Dalek-like
cameras which patrolled the No Man's Land between them
and the distant red, blue and silver set.

After a while an inexorably cheerful man, who introduced
himself as Charlie Hook, bounced on to the set and welcomed them. It was lovely to see so many smiling faces on
such a cold night, he asserted. He could see, just by looking
at them, that they were going to be a lovely audience, and
W.E.T. had got a really lovely show lined up for them that
evening. There were a few lovely parties he'd like to say hello
to. Was there a party from the Braintree Afternoon Club? Oh

50

yes, there they were! Well, a really big hello to them. Didn't they look lovely? And were they all set to have a lovely time? Good, yes, that was the spirit. Now, as he said, it was going to be a really lovely show, and to make the show really go with a swing, he wanted to hear lots of lovely laughter and applause from the lovely audience. Would they be lovely enough to oblige him? Good, yes, that was lovely. Now, of course, at W.E.T., they didn't have little men holding up signs saying "LAUGH" and "APPLAUD". What they were after was spontaneous reactions. On the other hand, there could be one or two moments when the audience might need to be told when these spontaneous reactions were required, her, her. So, if they saw him, Charlie, or one of the Floor Managers. . . . Ooh, they'd like to meet the Floor Managers, wouldn't they? Yes, of course they would. Lovely fellows they were, the Floor Managers, lovely fellows. And here they were. Say a lovely big hello. Lovely. So, anyway, if he, Charlie, or one of the Floor Managers raised their arms *like this*, would they please regard it as a cue to applaud and not a signal that they should leave the room, her, her. Lovely, right, good. Well, it would just be a few minutes before they got on with the show, so perhaps he could tell them a rather lovely story he'd heard a few days before about an Irishman who went into a café and ordered a hot dog. . . .

Eventually, Charlie Hook introduced their lovely host for the evening's proceedings, someone they all knew very well from countless other shows, one of the loveliest, most genuine people and one of the most popular faces on British Television—Mr—Barrett—Doran!

As soon as he came on to the set, Barrett switched his charm on like a light-bulb. He chatted with members of the audience, told them he felt terribly nervous, reiterated how important their contribution to the success of the evening would be, explained a little about the mechanics of the game and then introduced "our four celebrity guests, who will be playing *If The Cap Fits* with us tonight!"

The celebrities came on, with varying degrees of ostentation, and sat down behind their long blue desk. Barrett Doran told the audience that, once the show started, they would be meeting some delightful (and very plucky!) contestants who had also agreed to take part in *If The Cap Fits*. He then asked the Floor Manager how ready everyone was to start the recording. Had to check with "the boffins in the box", he explained to the audience. Terrific production team they'd got on the show. Great Executive Producer, John Mantle. Really talented Producer, Jim Trace-Smith. Really great back-up team, as well. All great chums, one big happy family. How about a nice round of applause for all those people out of sight whose contribution was so important in making the evening the success it was absolutely bound to be?

The audience duly applauded.

There were a few more delays, but finally the recording was ready to commence. Members of the audience were advised to watch the monitors rather than the set, because the opening credits were on film. The audience duly gawped up at their monitors. They saw the clock which was used to identify the programme. It was started and ticked away for sixty seconds. For the last three of these the screen went blank.

Animated credits of cartoon figures changing hats appeared. High-pitched jingle voices sang out the words as the title, *If The Cap Fits*, appeared in silver letters on the screen. A deep, unseen voice intoned portentously, "And tonight, on *If The Cap Fits*, our star prizes include . . . a portable video-recorder and lightweight camera . . ."

A shot of this hardware, carried by a grinning, bikini-clad Nikki, was shown on the screen. "Ooh," went the audience, and applauded.

". . . a champagne weekend for two in Amsterdam . . ."

An inappropriate clip of a Dutch windmill appeared. "Ooh," went the audience, and applauded.

". . . and tonight's super-duper star prize—a brand-new Austin Metro with all the extras, plus a full year's tax, insurance and petrol!"

The Austin Metro appeared on screen. Through its open window a grinning, bikini-clad Linzi waved awkwardly. "Aaaaah," went the audience, and applauded frantically.

More cartoon figures changed hats. "All these could be won tonight by some lucky contestant," the voice continued, "*if the cap fits*! And here's the man who wears a variety of hats with equal success . . . Barrett Doran!"

The show's host bounced, smiling, up to his lectern. The audience gave him an ovation which might have been warranted if he had just invented an antidote to radiation sickness.

"Hello, hello, and thank you very much. Welcome to *If The Cap Fits*. And if it doesn't, well . . . keep it under your hat! Thank you, thank you. And without more ado—nice girl, Moira Do, pity she couldn't be with us tonight . . . thank you—without Moira Do, let's meet our panel of celebrities who are going to find out for themselves tonight . . . *if the cap fits*!

"First, it's a great pleasure to welcome that lovely actress, who you all know as Lizzie Parsons from that very funny series, *Who's Your Friend?*—Fiona Wakeford!"

The actress simpered prettily in response to the applause.

"Tell me, Fiona," asked Barrett, "are you really as dumb as you appear?"

"Well, no," she replied, bewildered. "I can talk."

The audience screamed at this Wildean riposte.

"Next we have a gentleman who really packs a punch—Nick Jeffries!"

The audience saluted their faded Great White Hope.

"'Ere!" The boxer made a fist. "I don't like your attitude."

The audience hailed another shaft of wit.

"Actually, Barrett," Nick went on as the noise subsided, "that reminds me of a joke about a man with a dog. This bloke—"

"I make the jokes around here," said the host with a smile on his lips and a deterrent steeliness in his eyes. "Next, we have a lady who's brought happiness to millions—and without taking her clothes off, which has to be a novelty—the country's favourite Agony Aunt—Joanie Bruton!"

The audience roared as she smiled in a brisk, no-nonsense manner.

"Tell me, Joanie—or may I call you Auntie?—could you help me with a little personal problem that I have?"

"Perhaps, Barrett."

"Well, my trouble is that I keep thinking I'm a pair of curtains. What do you think I should do about it?"

"Pull yourself together, love." Joanie completed the old joke with commendable promptness and the audience howled their appreciation for this devastating sally.

"Finally, we have a gentleman who never seems to be off your television screen these days, investigating frauds, righting wrongs, standing up for the little man . . . you may know him as Joe Soap—Bob Garston!"

The last panellist gave his gritty, proletarian smile as the audience clapped.

"Tell me, Bob, have you ever come across a major fraud that involved hats?"

"No, you're the first one, Barrett."

The audience bayed with delight, honoured to be participants in this rare feast of wit. "Eat your heart out, Congreve," they seemed to say.

Barrett Doran's smile stayed in place, but the reaction of his eyes to Bob Garston's crack was less genial. "And now, as well as this splendid line-up of celebrities, we also have four brave—or should I say foolish?—members of the public who have agreed to be with us tonight to play *If The Cap Fits!*"

On this cue, one of the high-pitched jingles was played and, under cover of the music, the four contestants, propelled by the invisible Chita, moved awkwardly on to the set. Barrett Doran, scooping up a little pile of printed cards from his lectern, moved across to greet them effusively.

"Now first we have a very charming lady who's come all the way from Billericay. Patricia Osborne is her name, but she's known to her friends as Trish." He beamed the full force of his charm straight at her, and putting on a babyish voice, asked, "Can I be one of your friends and call you Trish?"

"Of course, Barrett."

"Terrific. Now I gather, Trish, that you're not the world's greatest decorator . . ."

"Not really, Barrett, no."

"In fact . . ." He consulted the card, on which the researchers had summarized the answers to the "any amusing incidents that may have happened in your life" part of their questionnaire. ". . . I gather you once papered your bedroom with vinyl wallpaper and woke up next morning to find it had all fallen off the walls on top of your bed!"

"That's right, Barrett," Trish agreed over the audience's hoots of delight.

"And I bet your husband said, 'Trish, that's the vinyl straw!'"

"No, he didn't actually." But Trish Osborne's response was lost in the audience's acclamation of their favourite epigrammatist.

The other three contestants were introduced with comparable wit, and then the rules for the First Round were explained. The four contestants were paired with their celebrity helpers. (A last ditch attempt by Tim Dyer not to be

55

landed with Fiona Wakeford was brutally thwarted.) Then, to the sound of another jingle, the hamburger chef, the surgeon, the stockbroker and the actor moved into their prearranged positions. The hamburger chef was wearing the Tudor bonnet, the surgeon the bowler, the stockbroker the chef's hat, and the actor the green hygienic cap. The camera moved slowly from one to the other, while the participants and audience tried to estimate which face went with which profession.

In turn, each contestant and celebrity team rearranged the hats to their satisfaction. Graphics superimposed over the picture recorded their guesses. It was all very riotous. Two out of the four contestants unhesitatingly identified Charles Paris as the hamburger chef.

To much oohing and aahing, Barrett Doran then gave the correct solutions. Contestants and celebrities responded with extravagant hand-over-face reactions to their errors. The four "professions" smiled fixedly as their true identities were revealed. The stockbroker was asked if she really was a stockbroker, the hamburger chef was asked to go easy on the onions, and the surgeon was asked if the first cut really was the deepest. The actor wasn't asked anything. The four were then fulsomely thanked for their participation and, as soon as the camera was off them, hustled unceremoniously off the set by a Floor Manager. At least one of them went straight to the bar and spent the rest of the evening there, risking topping up the earlier gins with Bell's whisky.

Which meant that Charles Paris didn't see the rest of that evening's rather unusual recording.

Points and money prizes were then awarded to the contest- ants. They got £50 for each correct hat. Two had scored a maximum of £200. One of these was Tim Dyer, who con- gratulated himself on his tactic of having ignored everything Fiona Wakeford said. The other was Trish Osborne. A third contestant scored £100. The fourth, who had managed to get them all wrong, was thanked by Barrett Doran for being a really good sport and asked if she had had a good evening. She assured him it had been the best of her life, before she was consigned to the outer limbo off the set. But, the audience was told, she would not be going away empty-handed. No, she would take with her a special *If The Cap Fits* cap, hand-made in red and blue velvet with a silver tassel. A shot of this artefact appeared on the audience's monitors and was greeted by the statutory "Ooh."

The three survivors were then detached from their cele-brity assistants for Round Two. The lovely Nikki and the lovely Linzi, still (for the most basic of audience-pulling reasons) dressed in bikinis, brought on four red-and-blue-striped hat-boxes which they placed on the long blue desk beside each panellist. Barrett Doran read out a list of five types of hat (one was a red herring), and asked the four celebrities in turn to read out a clue of mind-bending ambi-guity about the contents of their box. The contestants then had to hazard guesses as to which box contained which hat. The celebrities responded to these guesses with much elabo-rate bluffing, double-bluffing, tactical drinking from their water-glasses and heavy gesturing. Again, graphics recorded the contestants' final decisions and, at the end, Barrett Doran made his startling revelation of the truth. It was all very riotous.

Once again, £50 depended on each hat. With the red herring, that meant a possible total of £250, which Tim Dyer, much to his satisfaction, achieved. This win also earned him the portable video-recorder and camera. Trish Osborne had got two hats the wrong way round, so only won another £150. But she was still in contention. The third contestant, having identified only one hat correctly, departed from the show with £150 in winnings from his two rounds and, of course, with his *If The Cap Fits* cap.

"So," Barrett Doran asserted, "everything to play for after the break! See you in a couple of minutes, when once again it'll be time to see . . . *if the cap fits!*"

Barrett Doran left the set immediately the END OF PART ONE caption came up. Charlie Hook came forward to tell the audience what a lovely time they were having and what lovely people they were and how lovely the second part of the show was going to be. And weren't the panellists lovely? And the contestants. Lovely, really, lovely.

Then Jim Trace-Smith came on to the set. The Producer, Charlie Hook explained to the audience, needed some "cutaway shots". These were just reactions from some of the participants, which might have to be cut in later and would make editing the show a lot easier. Jim Trace-Smith only needed to do reaction shots with the two eliminated contestants; he'd do any others he needed at the end of the recording of Part Two. So the two failed candidates were hauled back on to the set, made to stand in fixed positions and asked to go through a variety of facial reactions—delight, annoyance, excitement, frustration, despair. Neither of them had much aptitude for it; they lacked the professional performer's ability to switch expressions at will; so the recording process took longer than it should have done.

But at last all was set for the restart. A Make-up girl flashed in with a final puff of powder for the face of Tim Dyer, on whom the pressure was showing in the form of sweat. The designer, Sylvian de Beaune, leapt on to the set for one last check of the position of the blue lectern. A Floor Manager escorted Barrett Doran back from his dressing room or wherever he had been. Charlie Hook gave the audience one last reminder that they were lovely, the clock was again started and the jingle and caption for PART TWO appeared.

Round Three was a simple General Knowledge round, though it was dressed up in a way that conformed with the hat theme of the rest of the show. The lovely Nikki and the lovely Linzi, still in their inevitable bikinis, entered carrying a large red-and-blue-striped box with a small opening at the top. Each of the surviving contestants had to reach into this box and pull out a hat. The hat dictated the subject on which they would be questioned. Once they knew the subject they were entitled to choose the celebrity guest who they thought best qualified to help them answer questions on that subject. They had five questions each. An incorrect answer gave the other player a chance at the question. Each question was worth £40, offering £200 for five correct answers (or, in the unlikely event of one contestant getting all five wrong and the other getting them all right, £400 for ten correct answers).

Trish Osborne pulled out a nurse's hat. This meant her questions would be on Medicine. Which of the celebrities, Barrett Doran asked, did she think would be best qualified to help her on that subject? Nick Jeffries volunteered his services, saying that he had always fancied nurses. Bob Garston said he'd got a badge for First Aid when he'd been in the Boy Scouts. It was all very riotous. Trish Osborne shrewdly chose to be helped by Joanie Bruton.

Tim Dyer's lengthy scrabbling in the box produced an opera hat. Nobody knew instinctively what subject this suggested, and Barrett Doran had to explain that it was the sort of hat worn by a first-nighter, so it meant Tim would be answering questions on the Theatre. So who was he going to have helping him? Well, it didn't seem too difficult to come up with an answer to that, did it . . . *when they actually had an actress on the panel*? Tim Dyer chose to be helped by Bob Garston.

"Right, so, Trish and Joanie, we start with you. And here's your first question: Which part of your body would be affected if you were suffering from galucoma? Glaucoma."

Joanie whispered to Trish.

"Your eye."

59

"Yes, that's right. Glaucoma is a disease of the eye. Well done. Forty pounds to add to your growing total, Trish. Over to Tim and Bob, and your questions, remember, are on the Theatre. Here's your first one: Who was the first actor ever to be knighted? The first actor ever to be knighted?"

A hurried consultation was followed by the answer, "Henry Irving."

"Henry Irving, good. Yes, that is the correct answer. Henry Irving became *Sir* Henry Irving in 1895. Well done. Back to the lovely ladies . . ."

It was nip and tuck all the way. Joanie and Trish missed out on their third question: How do you spell psittacosis?, but Bob and Tim couldn't do it either, so the scores remained level. The men couldn't get the answer to their third either. They didn't know which actress once played Hamlet with a wooden leg. Trish, prompted by Joanie, identified Sarah Bernhardt. One ahead.

The "lovely ladies" couldn't answer their fourth; nor could the men. But the men got their own fourth answer right, so, with one question each to go, the scores were once again level.

"Right, ladies. Your last question," said Barrett portentously, "who was the Roman God of Healing and Medicine?"

Trish Osborne looked totally blank. Joanie Bruton's pretty little brow wrinkled as she tried to dredge up some distant memory.

"Have to hurry you. Who was the Roman God of Healing and Medicine?"

Joanie whispered to her partner.

"Was it Hippocrates?" asked Trish tentatively.

"No, I'm sorry, it wasn't. The correct answer was Aesculapius. Aesculapius was the Roman God of Healing and Medicine."

A spasm of annoyance crossed Joanie Bruton's face. She

recognized the right answer and felt cross with herself for not having said it.

"So it's over to the gentlemen, for a question which could win for you, Tim, not only a nice lot of money to add to what you've already collected, but also a champagne weekend in Amsterdam to add to your video-recorder and camera. Not only that, if you get this question right, you will also take part in our *Hats In The Ring!* finale, with a chance to win this evening's Super-Duper Star Prize—the Austin Metro!"

The audience exhaled a long sigh of gratified materialism.

"So here is your last question on the subject of Theatre: From which of Shakespeare's plays does the following famous line come—'Once more unto the breach, dear friends, once more!'?"

Tim Dyer looked as if he knew, but, cautiously, he double-checked with Bob Garston. They both seemed to be in agreement.

"Henry V."

". . . is the right answer!" screamed Barrett Doran. The audience erupted into applause, through which another jingle played.

"Oh well done, Tim. Well done, Tim and Bob. But, ladies and gentlemen, a round of applause for our gallant loser. Thanks to Joanie Bruton, who nearly got her to the final, but not quite—and a big hand for Trish Osborne! Many thanks for playing the game, Trish. Have you had a good time?"

"Yes, thank you, Barrett, it's been really smashing."

"That's great. That's what we like to hear. And, of course, Trish isn't going to go back to Billericay empty-handed. No, she takes with her £470 and don't let's forget. . . ." He cued the audience to join in with him. ". . . her *If The Cap Fits* cap!"

Again the red, blue and silver creation appeared on the screen, as Trish Osborne was led off into the darkness.

Tim Dyer was looking very pleased with himself. All was

going according to plan. He had won everything he intended so far. Only the Austin Metro remained. Quietly confident, he prayed again to his own specialized God.

"Now, for the big *Hats In The Ring* finale. Tim, will you come over here." Barrett led the final contestant on to a little platform in the middle of the red spinning-wheel. "Now on to this wheel, as you see, a variety of hats are fixed." He pressed a button and the hats sprang into view. "Let's see, what have we got –an admiral's hat, a fez, a busby, a bishop's mitre. . . . Now each of these hats has a price marked on it, and that is the amount of extra money that Tim is going to win if that is the hat which, after the wheel has been spun, comes to rest above his head! So, you see, he gets £200 for the mitre, £500 for the busby, and so on. . . .

"Now you'll notice, two of the hats haven't got any price marked on them. There they are—right next door to each other—the dunce's hat and the crown! Now if the dunce's hat comes to rest above your head, Tim, I'm very sorry, but you get absolutely nothing extra."

"Ooh," sighed the audience, contemplating a fate worse than death.

"If, on the other hand, it's the crown, you, Tim Dyer, will instantly become the proud owner of a brand-new Austin Metro!"

"Aah," sighed the audience, reassured, and burst into spontaneous applause.

"Right, are you ready, Tim?"

The contestant, still praying and now glistening with sweat, nodded. All the lights faded except for those on the wheel and on Barrett's lectern.

"Here we go." Barrett held the edge of the wheel and gave it a hefty pull. It span wildly.

The host returned to his lectern and watched. Tim Dyer didn't move a muscle. The audience was totally still.

"Nerve-racking stuff, this," said Barrett Doran. "Tense moment."

He reached for the red-and-blue-striped glass in front of him.

The wheel showed little sign of slowing down. "Goes on for ever," said Barrett Doran jovially. "Dear, oh dear, the excitement's too much for me. Need a drink of water to calm me down."

He took a long swig from the glass.

The wheel was slowing. The audience started shouting at it, willing it to stop by the crown. Every eye was on a monitor, hypnotized by the decelerating ring of hats.

Suddenly they were all aware of a strange noise. It was a gasping, a desperate, inhuman wheezing.

A camera found Barrett Doran, from whom the sound came. The audience had time to register the face rigid with shock, before, pulling the lectern down with him, he crashed to the floor.

Full studio lights snapped up. Technicians rushed forward. The celebrities rose to their feet, overturning their long blue desk.

In the circle of hats Tim Dyer stood, pointing up at the still crown directly above his head. But no one looked at him. All eyes were drawn to the middle of the set, where Barrett Doran lay dead.

Chapter Five

CHARLES PARIS HEARD about Barrett Doran's death that evening. It was hard to escape it in the W.E.T. bar, where much less dramatic events were regularly inflated into Wagnerian productions. He heard that doctors and the police had been called, but had left W.E.T. House and was on his way back to his Bayswater bedsitter before anyone mentioned the word "murder".

The next morning the death was reported on radio and in Charles's *Times*, but it was not until the afternoon's edition of the *Standard* that it was suggested the incident might have been caused by anything other than natural causes. Two days later the press announced that a woman was helping the police with their enquiries into Barrett Doran's death, and the following day a 24-year-old employee of West End Television, Caroline Postgate, was charged with his murder. Then, as always with British crimes, all information on the case would cease until the trial.

The girl's name meant nothing to Charles, but, having been virtually on the spot when the murder happened, he felt intrigued by it and wanted to find out more. His first move was to contact his agent. Maurice Skellern, though completely deaf to vibrations of new productions coming up which might lead to jobs for his clients, had a very good ear for theatrical gossip, and was likely to know as much as anyone about a juicy theatrical murder.

Still, first things first. Charles asked the mandatory question about whether there was any work coming up.

Maurice Skellern laughed wheezily down the phone, as if this was the best joke he had heard for a long time. He did not answer the question; nor did Charles really expect him to. He knew that, on the rare occasions when something did come up, his agent would ring him.

Maurice was quickly on to the real subject of the conversation. "Had a bit of excitement the other night at W.E.T., I gather."

"You could say that."

"You got any dirt on it to tell me?"

"'Fraid not. I was ringing you in search of the same."

"But come on, Charles. You were actually *there*."

"Up in the bar."

"So what else is new? So how much do you know?"

"Just that he died on the set at the end of the recording, and now some girl I've never heard of has been charged with his murder."

"Well, what can I tell you? For a start, he was poisoned. Did you know that?"

"No. With what?"

"Cyanide."

"Ah." One or two things began to fall into place. "Cyanide which was being used for the programme in the studio next door?"

"You have it in one. Something that boring little poseur Melvyn Gasc was doing, apparently. Seems the cyanide got nicked from there and put into poor old Barrett's glass instead of water."

"Gin."

"What?"

"Instead of gin. Barrett's water-glass on the set was filled with gin."

"Was it? How do you know that?"

Discretion dictated a slight editing of the next reply. "One of the researchers was talking about it. So presumably this

65

girl who's been arrested was the one who substituted the cyanide?"

"Yes."

"Caroline Somebody-or-other. Know anything about her?"

"She was an Assistant Stage Manager on Melvyn Gasc's programme. She had been left in charge of all the props and that, so it was easy for her to lift the cyanide."

"Ah." Light began to dawn. "Was this girl nicknamed Chippy?"

"That's right. Why, you know her?"

"I met her that night."

The girl's beautiful, fragile face came into his mind. So, when he saw her, she had been contemplating murder. Perhaps that explained the tragedy in her deep, dark eyes.

"Needless to say, there was a background," Maurice went on. "She and Barrett had been having an affair. He had just broken it off. Classic situation. 'Hell hath no fury . . .', all that."

"Yes," Charles agreed pensively.

"Not a lot more I can tell you," his agent concluded. "Though I gather, talking to people in the business, nobody's that sorry. Barrett Doran doesn't seem to have made many friends on his way to the top."

"Having seen him in action, I'm not too surprised."

"No. Presumably means they'll have to remake the pilot. Wonder if you'll get booked again . . ."

"Not if anyone's got any sense. It was a daft idea having an actor as one of the people in that round."

"Ah, but nobody has got any sense in the game-show world."

"You mean otherwise they'd be doing something else?"

"Stands to reason, doesn't it? Anyway, why do you say it's such a daft idea having an actor for the round?"

"Because the whole premise of that part of the game is

based on people's anonymity, and actors, by definition, aren't anonymous. They're always in the public eye."

"Are you saying somebody recognized you?"

Charles was forced to admit that this had not been the case.

"But, come the game, you mean subconsciously they all recognized you and all identified you as the actor?"

Charles was forced to admit that two out of the four contestants had thought he was a hamburger chef.

Maurice Skellern thought this very funny. His asthmatic laughter was still wheezing down the line when Charles said his goodbyes and put the phone down.

He stood for a moment on the landing of the house in Hereford Road. He was feeling shaken. Not by the news of the murder, but by the thought of his illicit sips of gin from Barrett Doran's glass. A little bit later and his thirst might have killed him. It was an unpleasant *frisson*.

He wondered whether he should ring his wife and tell her how close he had come to death. His relationship with Frances was once more in the doldrums. They had long ago separated, but ties remained and, like two pieces of wood floating down a river, they occasionally bounced back together again for brief periods. The love between them was too strong for either to form other permanent relationships, but soon after each reconciliation, the same old difficulties of living together reasserted themselves, and once again they would drift apart.

It had been a couple of months since their last such parting and, though he knew nothing would have changed, Charles needed to make contact again. Perhaps hearing that he had nearly swallowed a fatal dose of cyanide would make Frances forget their recent disagreements. It would be a good opening gambit, anyway.

He looked at his watch. No, of course not. It was a quarter to twelve in the morning. Frances was headmistress of a girls' school. She wouldn't mind his ringing her there in a real

67

emergency, but just to mention casually that he'd nearly been poisoned . . . forget it.

On the other hand, at that time of day the pubs would be open. After his shock, Charles felt he deserved a little pampering. He went down to his local and had a few pints. By the third he had forgotten about the idea of ringing Frances. And, if he thought anything about Barrett Doran's death, it was only pity for the beautiful, sad girl who had been driven to such extremities by love.

And, but for a phone-call he received the next morning, he might have never thought any more about it.

The pampering of the previous lunchtime had escalated into evening pampering in various pubs and clubs where Charles always felt confident of meeting other actors. As a result, he was moving somewhat tentatively around his bedsitter, as if his exploding head was unattached and had to be balanced between his shoulders, when the telephone on the landing rang.

"Hello." He hadn't intended it to come out as a growl, but that was the only sound of which his voice was capable under the circumstances.

"Could I speak to Charles Paris, please?"

"This is he . . . him."

The caller then seemed to identify itself as "Sidney Danson", which did not immediately ring bells. His fuddled mind was slowly registering that it was an unusually high voice for a man, when she mentioned West End Television and he knew where he was.

"What can I do for you, Sydnee?"

"It's about Barrett Doran's death."

"Oh yes?"

"You know Chippy's been arrested and charged, don't you?"

"I had heard."

68

"Well, I don't think she did it. I just can't imagine her . . . not killing him."

"Ah."

"Could we get together and talk about it?" She spoke very directly, with the confidence of someone who spent most of her working life on the telephone.

"We can meet if you like, but I don't think I'm going to be a lot of help to you. I didn't see anything. I was only in the studio for that first round."

"I still think you could help."

"Hmm. Have you any reason for thinking Chippy didn't do it?"

"Instinct."

"Not always very reliable, I'm afraid, instinct. The police aren't fools. On the whole, they don't make an arrest until they've got a pretty good case worked out."

Sydnee did not answer this objection. "I'd like to talk about it," she persisted.

"Okay. When do you want to meet?"

"Could you make it for a drink this evening after work?"

Charles was again reminded of how most people's lives were defined by the boundaries of work, while at times the only structure in his own seemed to be imposed by licensing hours, but he didn't comment. "Sure."

"Say . . . half-past six?"

"Fine. Where, down at W.E.T.?"

"No. Better off the premises. Too many people with their own theories down here. Do you know Harry Cockers?"

"I beg your pardon?"

"Cocktail bar. Covent Garden. Just off Floral Street."

"I'm sure I could find it. What, there at six-thirty?"

"Yes."

"One thing, Sydnee. . . ."

"Yes?"

"Why did you get in touch with me?"

"One of the Stage Managers here mentioned you. Mort Verdon . . . you remember him?"

"Sure."

"He said you'd sorted a few things out when those murders happened on the *Strutters* series."

Charles felt childishly pleased as he put the phone down. He was amused by the idea that, while his acting career remained undistinguished, his reputation as an amateur detective was spreading.

The venue currently called Harry Cockers had been through many identities in the previous decade, as various kinds of bars and restaurants became fashionable. Its latest manifestation was very Thirties, with bright jagged lines along every surface, and wall-panels showing geometrically-stylized silhouettes of dancing figures in evening-dress. Overhead large fans swished.

It was full at that hour, and as he gazed at the clientele crowding the long bar, Charles felt infinitely old. The variegated flying-suits, the strident colours of fabrics and hair, the lurid make-up which would have been condemned at Drama School as "horribly over the top", all seemed to point up the incongruity of his crumpled figure in its loyal sports jacket.

He needn't have worried. The bright young things at the bar were far too involved in themselves and each other to notice him as he peered from flying-suit to flying-suit, trying to identify Sydnee.

She wasn't there. At least, she wasn't there unless she had dyed her hair another colour (which was of course not impossible). He sat at an empty table on the outskirts of the action. If she was there, she could find him. He knew his own appearance hadn't changed in the last few days (or probably the last few decades).

He was gratified to discover that his invisibility did not

extend to the staff. He had hardly sat down before a waiter, whose tail-coat and white tie seemed at odds with the yellow-and-green-striped hair and the Christmas Tree decoration dangling from the ear-lobe, materialized to take his order. He drew Charles's attention to the infinite list of highly-priced cocktails on the card in front of him.

"Er, just a large whisky, please."

"On the rocks?"

"Please."

The waiter vanished, very quickly to return with a tall glass so full of ice that the whisky had paled almost to invisibility, and a large bill.

Charles sipped his drink, while mortifying thoughts about how old and out of touch he was ran through his head.

Sydnee's hair was still the same copper-beech colour when she appeared a few minutes later. Her flying-suit this time was electric blue.

"Hi," she said, offering no apology for her lateness. Television time, Charles remembered, except for the unshakable rigidity of studio schedules, is always approximate.

"Can I, er . . . ?" He looked round for the waiter.

But she had already snapped her fingers to summon one, ordered herself a Screwdriver and "another of the same" for him. Charles wasn't used to being with these thoroughly emancipated women.

Sydnee didn't bother with small talk, but went straight to the point. "I'm convinced Chippy didn't kill Barrett, but I want you to prove that she didn't."

"Is she a close friend of yours?"

"Fairly close, yes. We've worked on a lot of shows together. Been off on a few long locations. You get to know people pretty well stuck for a wet six weeks in a hotel in Scotland."

Charles nodded. There were people he had got to know pretty well in similar circumstances.

"And, from what you know of her character, you don't see her as a murderer?"

"No way."

"What is she like?"

"Well, she's dramatic and she's neurotic. Started as an actress before she went into stage management, so she tends to make a big production of everything. Also, looking like she does, she always has plenty of men after her . . ."

"But she's one of those girls who always ends up falling for the ones who are complete shits."

"Right." Sydnee looked at him appraisingly, but with approval, respecting his judgement. As he had on the day of the recording, Charles caught a momentary glimpse of the real person beneath the surface efficiency.

"And Barrett Doran was the latest in this long line of shits?"

Sydnee nodded.

"How long had it been going on?"

"Maybe six months on and off. They met on another W.E.T. series. Another game show, actually. Chippy was A.S.M. on that."

"They didn't move in together?"

"No. He'd just turn up at her flat every now and then. Usually not when he said he would. She spent a lot of those evenings sitting waiting with the dinner slowly drying up in the cooker. Then another night he'd turn up at one in the morning with no warning at all."

"How to win friends and influence people."

"Oh, Chippy lapped it up. There was always a kamikaze element in her relationships. She asked for it."

"And she got it."

"Yes."

"Barrett presumably had other fish to fry?"

"You bet. He was the worst sort of celebrity. Reckoned,

because he was a famous face, he could get off with anyone. And usually he could."

"Did Chippy mind that?"

"At first I think she did. Then she realized that either she would have to accept all the others or forget it, so she stopped complaining. I think it kind of fuelled her masochism."

"Was Barrett married?"

"Not significantly. I think there probably was a wife somewhere in the background, but it didn't inhibit his activities."

"And, if Chippy was prepared to put up with all that, why was she suddenly reckoned to be capable of murdering him?"

"Because he broke it off. Didn't just stop turning up at her flat, didn't just stop ringing her . . . he actually told her: Forget it, it's all over."

"Any idea why?"

"I think he was probably just bored with her. The sex, from her account, was pretty good, but then he could get plenty of sex elsewhere. I think also Chippy was a bit ordinary for him."

"What do you mean?"

"Just an Assistant Stage Manager. Little bit of fluff, little bit of nothing. Barrett was getting to that stage of celebrity where he no longer just wanted to screw everything in sight, he only wanted to screw other celebs. You know, he wanted to be seen around with people, wanted to make it to the gossip columns."

"And Chippy didn't match up?"

"No. Not famous enough."

"Hmm. Sounds as if she was well shot of him."

"Yes, of course she was. I told her it'd be a disaster from the start. Trouble was, Chippy reckoned she had fallen in love with him—no, let's be fair to her, she *had* fallen in love with him. I mean, I know she always dramatized things, but this time it was a bit different. I'd seen her in the throes of other affairs, but she had never been like she was with Barrett. She was just totally obsessed with him. She used to tape all his shows and sit at home on her own watching them."

"What, game shows?"

"Yes."

"She'd sit and watch game shows for pleasure? My God, it must have been love."

Charles stopped short. He remembered that he was talking to someone whose work was game shows. He mustn't assume that she shared his cynicism on the subject, and be careful that he didn't offend her.

Sydnee's pale-blue eyes stared at him for a long, uncomfortable moment. Then, slowly, a childlike smile broke across her face.

"It's all right, Charles. I'm fully aware of the real quality of what I work on. But the work is nothing to do with the end-product. As you know, you can still be satisfied with your own professional contribution to a project that is utter rubbish."

He nodded. He had frequently had that experience. There was now more of a bond between them.

His glass was empty. He looked around vaguely, but again a peremptory gesture from Sydnee produced the waiter and repeated their order.

"Presumably," he said, picking up the threads, "Chippy's obsession with Barrett is one of the reasons why the police reckon she killed him?"

"Yes. Oh, she was certainly doing all the classic things a murder suspect should . . . going round saying what a bastard he was, how much she hated him, how much she wished he'd never existed. I mean, none of us could deny that she had issued plenty of threats against him."

"You were questioned by the police?"

"Oh yes. Everyone who was on the set at the time of the murder."

"I'm surprised they haven't been on to me."

"They've got your address and phone number. I just don't think they needed to spread the net any wider. They reckon they've got enough to convict Chippy already."

"Hmm. Like what?"

"Well, let's say we've sorted out Motive. As I recall from my teenage reading of detective stories, the next point to be checked was always Opportunity."

"That's right."

"So far as Opportunity was concerned, Chippy was uniquely placed. She was working on *Method In Their Murders*, she knew Melvyn Gasc had insisted on the realism of having all the correct props for the series, so she knew that the bottle of cyanide was around."

"And she went off to look after Studio B soon after six. I remember."

"Exactly. So she had a unique opportunity to doctor Barrett's glass."

"Which contained gin originally, am I right?"

"Yes. How did you know?"

Again Charles fudged the truth a little. "I worked it out from things Barrett said to you."

"He always insisted on his glass of gin. Don't blame him, actually. You need something to keep up that relentless good humour in front of the camera."

"Hmm. One strange thing that struck me," Charles mused, going off at a tangent, "was why he didn't die earlier."

"Sorry? I'm not with you."

"Well, if he was that dependent on the gin, why didn't he take a big swig earlier on in the recording? Why did he wait till the end?"

"Yes, I wondered about that. The only reason I could think was that, under all that brashness, Barrett Doran was very nervous. He was concentrating so hard on getting the new show right that he forgot about the booze."

"I suppose that's possible."

"He did nip off to his dressing room for a big one at the end of Part One."

"Ah."

"Also, he played it well. I mean, in terms of drama. He only used the drink when the wheel was spinning, claiming that he couldn't stand the tension. He was a good showman, Barrett."

"Hmm." Charles took a long, pensive swallow of whisky. "Did you get a chance to talk to Chippy after the recording?"

"Yes, I did. We went out for a few drinks after the first round of police questioning."

"What sort of state was she in?"

"Pretty terrible. Kind of numb and totally fatalistic. Like part of her was dead. With Barrett gone, she didn't reckon she had anything to live for. That's what worries me. If she's in that sort of state, she's not going to fight. I know her. She'll just accept being accused of the murder. She'll see it as a kind of punishment, yet another proof that it's a rotten world and she never had a chance."

"But she can't just have been charged on circumstantial evidence. The police must have got a bit more on her."

"Yes, I suppose they have. You see, she did fiddle around with Barrett's glass."

"Did she?"

"Oh yes. She made no bones about it. She told me that evening. And presumably she told the police too."

"What did she say she did?"

"While she was meant to be looking after Studio B in the meal-break, she was feeling really vindictive towards Barrett—you know, particularly after he'd cut her dead in the bar—and she decided she'd have a small revenge on him. She knew about the gin, knew he always had a glass on the set, so she just thought she'd deprive him of that comfort.

She said all she was going to do was to change his glass round with one of the others on the celebs' desk."

"Did she say whose?"

"No. Anyway, she says she didn't do it. When she got into the studio, she picked up the glass, then realized how petty she was being and didn't bother."

"She just left things as they were?"

"So she said. Well, the police ran fingerprint checks. Needless to say, hers were all over the cyanide bottle—she'd been handling the Studio B props all day. They were also all over Barrett's glass and decanter—along with a lot of other prints."

"Oh really?" said Charles innocently.

"So, given that evidence, and her motive, and the fact that she and Barrett had a shouting match just before the recording. . . ."

"Did they?"

"Yes. She went to his dressing room, silly girl. Shouted all kinds of things that a lot of people heard. Said how he wouldn't get away with the way he'd treated her, how she had planned how to get even with him. . . ."

"Direct threats?"

"That's it, I'm afraid."

Charles looked down at the melting ice of his drink. His conclusion was inescapable, but he wanted to phrase it as gently as possible.

"Listen, Sydnee, I know Chippy's a friend of yours and I can see exactly why you're doing what you're doing, why you're involving me, but I'm afraid it does sound pretty hopeless. I mean, Chippy had every reason to want Barrett dead, and she had the opportunity to kill him. From what you say of her mental state, she sounds to have been quite hysterical enough to have done it. I'm sorry, Sydnee, but I think the police are right. They've got their murderer."

The pale blue eyes were full of pain. To his surprise, he saw tears gathering at their corners.

"As I say, I'm sorry, but that's how it must have happened. She went to Barrett's dressing room, hoping for the final reconciliation. He was as unpleasant to her as ever. She thought, all right, sod the bastard, I'll get him. She went back to Studio B, got the bottle of cyanide . . . into Studio A and filled his glass. Wouldn't have taken her more than a minute. And that was it."

Sydnee was silent for a moment. Then, softly, she said, "Except it wasn't."

"What do you mean?"

"I heard about the argument going on in Barrett's dressing room, and I went down to get Chippy out of it. I then took her back to the bar and bought her a large drink. So she's got an alibi from the time she went into Barrett's dressing room."

"Okay, so she must have doctored the drink before she went to see him. It doesn't make a lot of difference to the main outline of the crime. She told him she was going to get him."

"Yes."

Sydnee's reply was so listless, and she looked so dejected, that Charles felt he must summon up a little more interest.

"Let's look at the time-scale. When did she say she went into Studio A to switch the glasses?"

"First thing she did when she went down from the bar. And that's when the police say she put the cyanide in the glass. It was the only chance she had. She was seen going into Barrett's dressing room at twenty-five-past six, and I got her out of there about twenty to seven."

Charles did the sums in his head. Then, slowly he said, "Ah. You know, Sydnee, I think you may have a point, after all."

Because, as he knew well (and with a degree of gratitude), at six-thirty the contents of the glass on Barrett Doran's lectern had been not cyanide, but gin.

Chapter Six

IT WAS THE first time Charles had had the privilege of his own research team in investigating a murder. Sydnee had mustered all of the researchers who had worked on *If The Cap Fits* to go through the events of the day Barrett Doran died. In an unguarded moment, when they had been trying to think of somewhere private to meet, Charles had suggested his bedsitter. He had not taken into account the fact that he had only two chairs. Nor had he thought through the reaction of these television sophisticates to his somewhat approximate view of tidiness.

None of them was impolite enough to say anything, but he sensed a sniff of disapproval in the air. Their standards were probably different from his. In domestic arrangements, Charles always made a distinction between hygiene and tidiness. And, though he knew he offended against the strict canons of the second, he felt confident that he did not transgress with regard to the first.

Assuming, of course, that one didn't regard dust as unhygienic.

There was a generous cover of dust over every surface. And, since none of these surfaces were flat, but tended to be piles of books, clothes, stationery and scripts, the general effect could be, to the uncharitable eye, seen as a mess.

This view seemed to be reflected in his visitors' expressions. Sydnee sat on a chair. The other girl, Chita, who had been responsible for the contestants on the studio day, had the other one. Charles shared the edge of the bed with the rather exquisite young man called Quentin, who had been in charge of the celebrities. Charles had offered whisky and wine; they had all chosen white wine. He had some chilling (a little belatedly—he'd only thought about it ten minutes before they arrived) in his small fridge, and had soon assembled a whisky tumbler, a half-pint tankard and a chipped glass that had been given away with soap powder for his guests. He was left with a pink plastic tooth-mug for his whisky.

The atmosphere was not unfriendly, though the three researchers seemed to be suffering mild disbelief at the idea of people actually living in such surroundings. Charles thought it might be only a matter of time before they started making a documentary about him.

Sydnee opened the meeting. "Chita and Quentin are fully up-to-date with everything. They're as concerned as I am to get the charges against Chippy dropped."

"Have you mentioned to them the idea of going to the police?" Charles asked formally.

"Yes. We're all agreed that we shouldn't do that until we can point the finger at the person who really killed Barrett."

"But surely . . . if all you want is to get Chippy free, all I have to do is go and tell the police that Barrett's glass still contained gin at half-past six and—"

"No." Sydnee was implacable. "Apart from anything else, that's then going to start the police being suspicious of you. We need your help; we don't want you shut up in a cell 'helping the police with their enquiries'."

Charles agreed. It was an aspect of the situation he hadn't considered. So . . . he was committed to the case now. He'd better accept it with good grace.

"Right, so let's see where we are. We know that Barrett Doran's glass contained gin at six-thirty. What time would everyone start coming back from their meal-break? Sharp at seven?"

"Most people would, yes," said Sydnee. "Cameras have to line up for half an hour between seven and seven-thirty, so the cameramen would drift back at around five to."

"But the P.A. would probably have been in the Gallery before that," Quentin contributed. And there might be other people drifting back a bit earlier . . . Stage Managers, people checking props . . ."

Chita agreed. "Yes. It'd be quite a risk to try to do anything criminal after about ten to. Likely to be someone around then."

"So we've narrowed down the time when the cyanide was put in the glass to the twenty minutes between six-thirty and ten to seven," Charles summed up. "Now, assuming that the murderer was someone connected with the show, which of your charges were out of your sight during that period?"

"I'll start," said Sydnee, "because my bit's probably the simplest. After I sent you down to Make-up, Charles, I was intending to send the other 'professions' down at five-minute intervals, but then I had a call in the bar from one of the Make-up girls saying they were getting behind and could I hold it. So your three fellow-performers didn't leave the bar till after seven."

"Are you sure? Because you went down to Barrett's dressing room at twenty to."

"I'm sure. I left them in the charge of a friend up in the bar. He confirmed none of them left. He was a bit pissed off, actually . . . found he had to buy them all a round of drinks."

So that ruled out the hamburger chef, the surgeon and the stockbroker.

"What about the contestants?" Charles asked Chita.

"Most of them stayed up in the Conference Room right through the meal-break. There were sandwiches and drink up there."

"When did they go to Make-up?"

"Not till about ten to seven. They didn't need much. Just a quick slap of foundation and powder."

"You said 'most of them' . . . ?"

"Yes, a couple went out about quarter past six, but they were both back by twenty to seven."

"Which ones?"

"The two who got through to the second half. The one who won. . . ."

"Tim Dyer," said Sydnee.

"And the housewife, Trish Osborne . . ."

"Madame Nipple," murmured Quentin.

Charles ignored this. "Where did they go to, Chita?"

"Well, they *said* they both fancied a steak and went down to the canteen . . ."

"But we've talked to Rose on the Grill Counter," Sydnee picked up the story, "who's got about the beadiest eyes in the business, and she's certain they didn't go in there."

"Ah. Well, there's two who might be worth investigating. But you're sure the others stayed put?"

"I was with them all the time," Chita confirmed.

"Right," said Charles. "On to the celebrities."

Quentin let out a languorous sigh. "Well, now, what can I tell you? We too were all cosy in our little Conference Room with lavish supplies of W.E.T. booze and W.E.T. sandwiches. There was a bit of toing and froing to dressing rooms . . ."

"Can you be more specific about this toing and froing?"

"Well . . . Fiona Wakeford 'toed' into her dressing room at about six-fifteen, and Nick Jeffries 'toed' into it at about six-sixteen. And she 'froed' him out at about six-seventeen." Quentin giggled at his little joke. "Then she stayed in her dressing room until seven putting her hair in the Carmen rollers."

"Are you sure about that?"

"Pozz. One of my friends is a dresser, and she called him

82

in to help her just after Nick left. For protection, too, I think."

"Nick?"

Quentin nodded. "He'd been chatting her up quite shamelessly all afternoon. I think when he went into her dressing room and actually put his hand on something, even dear Fiona realized he was after a bit. So she . . . 'froed' him out." He repeated the joke, maybe hoping for more reaction the second time. He didn't get it.

"So, although Fiona's out of the running, Nick was on the loose from six-twenty-two until . . . when?"

"Only about six-thirty, I'm afraid. He was back up in the Conference Room by then, downing a large Scotch to soothe his wounded ego. He certainly wasn't in the studio area for the vital twenty minutes."

"Sure?"

"Pozz."

"What about the other two panellists?"

"Well now. . . ." Another dramatic sigh was emitted. "Joanie went down to Make-up at about ten-past six."

"With her husband?"

"Oh yes, the faithful Roger was in tow."

"Did he go into Make-up with her?"

"Apparently not. Perhaps even he thought that would have been taking devotion too far."

"So he was on the loose down near the studios. Perhaps he should go on the list . . . ?"

"Uh-uh." Quentin shook his head. "Sorry, like Nick, they were back up in the Conference Room by half-past."

"Ah. So that rules both out."

"'Fraid so. I had my beady little eyes on the pair of them for every second of the vital twenty minutes. Not a sight I relished, I must confess," Quentin admitted with slight petulance. "I can only take so much connubial bliss, you know."

83

"What about Bob Garston?"

"Now he is much more interesting. Or, at least, his movements are much less well-documented. He was out of the Conference Room from about five-past six until twenty to seven. And no sightings, I'm afraid. Except that he was seen going down in the lift towards the basement, where the studios are. So he should certainly go on your little list."

"Right. Three names, then. Three who had the opportunity." Charles mused. "Of course, we've limited it enormously. We've only dealt with the ones directly concerned with the show. I mean, there are so many people around a television studio. It could have been any of them. Even someone working on a different programme . . ."

"Like Chippy was . . ." said Chita.

But Sydnee wasn't going to let them get depressed by logistics. "We've got to start somewhere," she pronounced. "Now, next thing we ought to think about motives."

"I'll tell you who had the biggest motive," said Quentin. "Those two Americans. You know, the one who kept talking about 'making a pot' and his tall, quiet friend. They were convinced that Barrett was ruining their precious show."

"Did they have the opportunity?"

Quentin shook his head wistfully. "Sorry, Charles. They spent the whole of the meal-break bending John Mantle's ear in the bar. Lots of witnesses for that."

"What about the other three then, the ones on the list? How're we doing for motive there?"

Sydnee took over. "Well, no one liked Barrett much. We know that. But who disliked him enough to murder him? . . . that's a different question. What does drive someone to murder? Presumably it varies from person to person. I mean, Barrett really humiliated Trish."

"You mean that business about her . . . her blouse?"

"Yes. He reduced her to tears in front of everyone. And she didn't seem to me to be the sort who cries easily."

"No."

"A lot of women would take that pretty hard. Whether hard enough to commit murder . . . I don't know."

"Won't dismiss it out of hand. What about the other contestant?"

"Tim Dyer's different. He was just totally obsessed by winning. And I mean *obsessed*. He's been on the phone every day since the recording."

"About what?"

"About the car. What he describes as *his* bloody car. He maintains that the crown had definitely stopped over his head at the end of the *Hats In The Ring* finale, and that, regardless of the fact that Barrett Doran was at that moment dying, the Austin Metro should be his. W.E.T., in the person of John Mantle, takes a different view."

"I'm not surprised. But do you reckon he had any motive against Barrett?"

"He was certainly extremely angry when Barrett paired him with Fiona Wakeford for Round One. He didn't reckon she was going to be much help to him."

"One can see his point," Quentin murmured.

"But whether you'd murder someone for that . . ."

Charles shrugged. "As you say, he was obsessed. Depends on the depth of his obsession, I suppose. What about Bob Garston?"

"I don't think he *liked* Barrett," Sydnee replied, "but then who did? There was also, I suppose, a professional rivalry."

"Oh?"

"Bob was considered for the job."

"Hosting the show?"

"Yes."

"And he knew that?"

"'Fraid so. He shouldn't have done, but he did. Casting Director was a little indiscreet with his agent when checking availability."

"And would he have wanted it?"

"I think so."

"'Course he would, Sydnee," said Quentin. "Just the sort of break he needs. Lose the 'reporter' tag. Become a 'personality'. A future of infinite chat-shows. He'd love it."

"And, of course, he may yet get it," said Chita.

"How do you mean?"

"There's a reasonable chance he'll be booked as host on the second pilot."

"Is there going to be a second pilot?"

"You bet," Sydnee replied. "W.E.T. shelled out a lot for the rights in that show. They're not going to let something minor like a murder stop them from capitalizing on it."

Charles bit back the actor's instinctive question ("If there is a second pilot, am I likely to be booked again?"), and said, "So he stood to gain very directly from Barrett's death. We should definitely investigate Bob Garston."

"Him first?"

"I'm not sure. I think we should try and see all three of them. Who's going to be the easiest to get in touch with?"

Sydnee laughed. "Tim Dyer. He's desperate for someone to go and talk to him about his bloody car."

Charles Paris grinned round at his research team. "Then maybe we should start with Tim Dyer."

Chapter Seven

SYDNEE DROVE AN old red MG Midget, fast. The hood was up, against the autumn weather, and she and Charles travelled in their noisy cocoon out along the A3 towards Petersfield, where their first suspect lived.

"Are you sure he's not going to think it odd, me coming along with you?" asked Charles.

"I don't think he'll give it a second thought. The only thing on his mind is that bloody Austin Metro."

"Is that what you said you wanted to talk about when you rang?"

"No, I didn't say it, but I think that's the way he took it. Wouldn't occur to him that there was anything else *to* talk about."

"Could be the second pilot."

"Could be, I suppose. Though, if the truth were known, he's very unlikely to be involved in that."

"Oh?"

"It's a matter of research time. It's difficult getting contestants, but it was more difficult setting up the rest of the programme. Probably be better to leave all that intact and just slot in four new contestants."

"What, leave the rest of the show just as it was?" asked Charles, scenting another booking.

"Yes. Assuming the powers-that-be don't want major changes in the format."

"Are they likely to?"

"Who can say? John Mantle and the American copyright-holders are watching the tape through today."

Charles grimaced. "Fairly grisly experience."

"Only the end. Up to there the show ran as it should. Very few recording breaks, it was fine. John Mantle won't waste the recording. I mean, for him it'll be great, having the luxury of a second pilot. Another bite of the cherry, a chance to make sure it's all dead right."

Charles winced. "*Dead* right."

"Sorry."

"Has it been decided yet whether Bob Garston will host it second time around?"

"Not definitely, no. I think it's a strong possibility."

"Hmm." Charles fell silent, his mind circling round the murder, round the possible motives and opportunities of its perpetrator.

They reached the outskirts of Petersfield. "Could you reach into my handbag? There's a sheet of W.E.T. notepaper where I wrote down the directions he gave me on the phone."

Charles complied and guided Sydnee towards their quarry. "What does he do?" he asked, as they turned into the road where Tim Dyer lived.

"He said on his form that he was a computer programmer."

"You sound sceptical."

"Yes. Just something about him sounds warning bells. Also, he said he'd be at home any time I cared to call."

"You mean you don't think he has a job?"

"Wouldn't surprise me."

"One of the unemployment figures? Made redundant, and too proud to admit it?"

"Possible." She didn't sound convinced. "Except that computers are one of our few boom industries. Wouldn't imagine there are that many redundant programmers."

"So what do you think?"

"I think he may have slipped through our net. I think he claimed to have a job just to put us off the scent."

"I'm still not with you."

"I rather suspect that Tim Dyer is one of those characters who all researchers try to spot and weed out. If I'm right, I'll kick myself for not having recognized it earlier."

Charles was mystified. "What sort of character?"

Sydnee stopped the car outside a neat, Thirties semi. In the drive stood a brand-new, gleaming Vauxhall Cavalier. She looked at Charles with a little grin as she pulled on the handbrake and replied, "A professional contestant."

It was clear as soon as they got inside the small front room that Sydnee had been right. Tim Dyer made no attempt to disguise what he did for a living. Indeed, he exulted in it. Perhaps, having played his part in *If The Cap Fits* and having, to his mind, won an Austin Metro from W.E.T., he saw no further necessity for secrecy.

He indicated a table, on which papers and open reference books lay between piles of cardboard coupons. "Doing another of the soap powder ones," he announced airily. "Pretty simple General Knowledge. Difficult bit's always the tie-breaker."

"Tie-breaker?"

"Bit at the end. Always a variation on the old 'I LIKE THIS PRODUCT BECAUSE . . . in not more than ten words.' Mind you, there is a knack to them," he added smugly.

"You've won in the past?" asked Charles. As Sydnee had predicted, Tim had registered no surprise, or indeed interest, at his presence.

"Just a few times." Tim Dyer smiled indulgently at the understatement. "Out of these I've won fifty pounds a week for life, three music centres, a food processor, a sailing dinghy and a fortnight's holiday for two in Benidorm."

"Good God. What do you do with all that lot?"

"Keep some. Sell a few. Though selling's always a pity, because you drop a lot on the price, even when it's brand-new. I prefer barter. I've got a good barter deal going with my local electrical shop."

"What did you do about the fortnight's holiday for two in Benidorm?"

"Oh, I went on that."

"Nice break for you and the wife."

"I'm divorced," said Tim Dyer. "No, I went, and sold the other half of the holiday to someone I used to work with. Had to drop the price a bit, but did all right. Trouble is, very few of the companies who put up these prizes are ready to give cash equivalent."

"Do you enter for everything?" asked Charles, bemused.

"Everything I hear about. And everything where there's a bit of skill involved. Like I say, there's a knack to it. The ones where it's pure lottery, it's not worth bothering, I've got no advantage over anyone else. Don't do any of those . . . well, except the *Sun* Bingo and *Times* Portfolio. Check them first thing every morning before I start on the rest."

"And you really find there are enough of them to keep you going?"

"You bet. In fact, I don't have time to do them all. I work weekends too, you know," Tim Dyer concluded piously.

"So you just sit here and—"

"Have to spend a lot of time in the supermarkets, checking the new promotions that are coming up, seeing what the competitions are, getting entry forms, coupons, buying up relevant stock."

"Relevant stock?"

"Come and have a look."

He led them through into what had presumably been intended as a dining room. But it contained no table and chairs. Instead, it was crammed full like a supermarket warehouse.

Tim Dyer gave them a conducted tour. He pointed to a ceiling-high pile of Cook-in-a-Bag Curry boxes, from each of which a side panel had been neatly cut. "Did all right out of that. Won a three-week holiday for two to India."

"Did you go on it?"

"No, sold it through the local paper." He indicated a wall of food cans, none of which had any labels. "Four different competitions, those were. Canned mangetouts, new instant custard launch, lychees in syrup and chile con carne. Got a yoghourt maker, cut-glass decanter set, tennis racket and two hair-dryers. Sold them all."

"Why no labels?"

He looked at Charles as if he were dealing with a moron. "They've got the coupons on. You have to get them off."

"Well, how can you tell whether it's instant custard or chile con carne?"

"You can't. I just open one and hope for the best."

"You do eat them?"

"I'm working through," said Tim Dyer, and pointed to a pile of washing-up powder boxes. These had also had coupons removed and powder spilled through the rectangular holes to make little peaks on the carpet. "Working through this lot, too. Good, though. Won a BMX bicycle on that. Sold it."

"How did you win the Vauxhall Cavalier?" asked Sydnee, who had been silent for a long time.

Tim Dyer looked at her sharply, realizing that the conversation had come round to something important. "Let's go into the front room."

When they were sitting, Sydnee persisted, "Where did you win the Cavalier?"

"Doesn't matter."

"I see. Another television show."

For a moment he looked as if he were about to deny it, but a slow, smug smile crept across his face. "Yes. Right. *Something For Nothing* I won that on."

"You've done a lot of other tellies."

91

He nodded slyly. "Oh yes. I've done most of them."

"Just a minute," said Sydnee, remembering something. "How did you get on *Something For Nothing*? That's a show for married couples."

"Yes."

"But you said you're divorced."

"I persuaded the wife to come back just for the show."

"And *you* got the car."

"Oh, come on. She got the fridge-freezer, the home computer with full range of software, the exercise bicycle plus His and Hers track-suits, the cordless telephone and the crate of vintage champagne."

"You still got the best of the deal."

"Well, I did the research, didn't I? And I answered all the questions."

"Erm . . ." Charles asked out of pure curiosity, "did appearing on the show together bring you and your wife back together at all?"

"Good God, no." Tim Dyer dismissed that idea and moved on to a subject that interested him more. "Now, about this Austin Metro . . ."

"Yes," said Sydnee, mentally girding up her loins for battle.

"I've taken legal advice on this, and my solicitor says it depends on whether the crown was definitely over my head when it stopped. Now I know it was, and that would be visible on the recording of the show that you have. If W. E.T. tries to withhold that tape, my solicitor says he would be able to—"

"We have also taken legal advice," Sydnee quelled him. "Our Legal Department has no precedent for this situation, but their view is that the rules of the game constitute a kind of verbal contract. In other words, W.E.T. has agreed to give away certain goods to contestants who fulfil the requirements demanded by the game."

"Exactly." Tim Dyer grinned hungrily. "Which I had done."

"However," Sydnee continued, "it is their view that this situation only lasts as long as the game continues, and they feel that the game cannot be said to continue after the death of the host."

"What!" He was furious. "But that's just cheating. Anyway, the crown had stopped over my head before he died."

She shook her head. "We've checked the tape. Barrett Doran definitely stopped moving before the wheel of hats did."

"I don't believe it. I demand to see the tape!"

"You're welcome to do so. Your solicitor is also welcome to do so. It won't change anything. The Austin Metro remains the property of West End Television."

Tim Dyer let out a terrible howl of frustrated materialism. "Cheats! You're just all cheats! I won that fair and square, and now you're saying I didn't! I'll fight it! I'll sue you! I'll get that car!"

"Try, by all means," said Sydnee equably, "but let me warn you, you're going into a very vague area of the law, and, as a general rule, the vaguer the area, the more expensive the law becomes."

Tim Dyer was silent, his mouth ugly with disappointment. He looked as if he had been winded by a blow to some vital part of his anatomy. And that was not far from the truth. He had just received a serious blow to his greed.

Charles judged it a good moment to move on to the real subject of their visit. "You didn't like Barrett Doran, did you?"

Tim Dyer looked surprised at this change of direction, but was still too much in shock to do anything but tell the truth. "No, I didn't. So?"

"Why did you dislike him? You'd only met him that afternoon, hadn't you?"

"Oh yes. But it doesn't take long to get the measure of someone like that." A glint of paranoia came into Dyer's eye, as he said, "He was out to stop me winning."

"What?"

"Oh yes. That bastard was out to nobble me from the moment we were introduced. He saw that I was the most likely contestant to win, and he was out to stop me."

"I don't think he was bothered with—"

"Oh, come on. Didn't you see the way he paired me off with that subnormal actress? It was quite deliberate. He was out to sabotage my chances." The paranoia gave way to satisfaction. "But I showed the bastard. I still won, didn't I?" The paranoia quickly reasserted itself. "Or I would have won if I hadn't been cheated of my car!"

"Listen . . ." Sydnee began, but, on a signal from Charles, she stopped.

"What did you do during the meal-break?" the actor asked suddenly.

Again he had judged it right. Tim was too surprised by the sudden demand to question why it should be asked. "Well, I . . . er . . . what do you mean?"

"You were in the Conference Room with Chita and the other contestants. You and Trish Osborne left there about quarter past six, and didn't get back till twenty to seven. You said you were going down to the canteen, but neither of you did. What were you doing?"

"Well, I wasn't with her, if that's what you were thinking," Tim replied truculently. "If she was getting off with anyone, it wasn't me. We only left the room together. We got in different lifts."

"Both going down?"

"I think so. Mine was, certainly."

"Which floor did you get off at?"

"I . . . . Look, what is this? Why are you giving me the

third degree in my own home? Who the hell do you think you are?"

"Someone's been murdered," Charles announced with all the chilling authority he had used in *Witness For The Prosecution* ("Profoundly unmoving"—*Plays and Players*).

"And someone's been charged with the murder."

"Yes. We happen to believe that the police have got the wrong culprit. Which is why we are checking what everyone was doing during the meal-break." By now he had slipped into the voice he had used as a Detective-Inspector (shortly to be killed) in a *Softly, Softly* ("A rather routine episode in this generally excellent series"—*New Statesman*). "So tell me exactly what you did when you left the Conference Room."

The Detective-Inspector manner had its effect. Tim Dyer spoke unwillingly, but at least he spoke. "I went down to the floor where the studios are. I just wanted to have a look round. I was nervous, you know, wanted to get on the set, get the feel of it. I thought it'd calm me down."

"And, once in the studio, what did you do?"

"I . . . well, I just looked round. You know, round the back."

"You looked at the displays of prizes?"

"All right. So what if I did? I needed to psych myself up for the show. I needed to sort of get the adrenalin going."

"So you went and gazed at the Austin Metro?"

"Yes," the contestant admitted sheepishly.

"And that's all you did?"

"Yes." But Tim Dyer would not look into his interrogator's eyes as he spoke.

"You were out of the Conference Room for twenty-five minutes. Sounds like a long time to look at a car."

"Well, I didn't go into the studio straight away."

"What, not immediately after you left the lift?"

"No. I was going in there, but I saw one of the celebrities

95

coming along the corridor and I didn't feel like chatting, so I turned into one of the phone booths along there till he'd gone past."

"Who was it?"

"Bob Garston."

"And he was coming from Studio A?"

"From that direction, certainly."

"This was straight after you came out of the lift?"

"Yes."

"So, say, twenty-past six?"

"Round then."

"Was Bob Garston on his own?"

"No, he was with Joanie Bruton's husband."

"Roger Bruton, eh?" Charles looked at Sydnee. "Who'd presumably just escorted his wife into Make-up." She nodded. "So, Tim, you just stayed in the phone booth as they walked past?"

"That's what I meant to do, but they stopped just outside and talked for a bit."

"Did you hear what they said?"

"Yes. It was strange. Bob Garston was saying, 'I didn't think anyone knew about it. Still, since you obviously do, you'll understand that I'm finding it pretty difficult to work in the same studio as the bastard.' And Roger Bruton said, 'Joanie's done a lot of counselling on infidelity in marriage. You ought to talk to her about it. She's very understanding.' And Bob said, yes, perhaps he would."

"And that was it?"

"Yes. Then they walked on."

"And you came out of the phone booth and went into Studio A?"

"Yes."

"To look at your car." Tim Dyer did not deem this worthy of comment, so Charles went on. "Did you see anyone in the studio?"

A twisted smile came to the contestant's lips. "Only you."

"Oh."

"I saw you swigging from his glass."

Charles blushed, but pressed on. "So you knew that it didn't contain cyanide at that point."

"Never occurred to me that it would. Why should I think that?"

"Somebody put cyanide in it between six-thirty and seven."

"Well, don't look at me. What do you take me for? I wouldn't do anything like that."

"No, I don't think you probably would." A new thought struck Charles. "Just a minute. You say you saw me drinking from Barrett's glass . . . ?"

"Yes."

"I didn't see you."

"So?" Tim Dyer looked uncomfortable.

"If you'd been behind the curtain round the back of the set, you wouldn't have been able to see me. If you'd been in the audience seating, I'd have seen you. That means you must have been out of sight, actually on the set."

"Well . . ." Tim Dyer began wretchedly.

"And the only thing on the set big enough to hide you would have been the spinning wheel." Suddenly Charles knew he was right. "You were behind that wheel . . . tampering with it."

"No, I wasn't." But the denial carried no conviction.

"Wouldn't take much, would it? All you needed to do was fix a counterweight on the wheel, directly opposite the crown, and that would guarantee it would always come to rest with the crown overhead. Simple."

Charles knew from the man's expression that he had inadvertently hit on the truth. Confidently, he asked one final question. "You didn't see anyone else in the studio after I left?"

Tim Dyer shook his head miserably and whispered, "I went out straight after you. Didn't see anyone else."

There was a long silence. Then Sydnee rose to her feet. "Better be going, I suppose."

Charles got up too, and they moved towards the hall. Just before they left the room, Sydnee looked back and said, "And, if you want to take up that point about cheating over the car, I suggest you get in touch with our Legal Department."

Tim Dyer did not respond. He stayed crumpled in his chair, looking as comically guilty as a schoolboy with stolen jam on his face.

Chapter Eight

SYDNEE RANG CHARLES the next morning. "You were right," she said.

"About what in particular?"

"Tim Dyer trying to fix the wheel. I spoke to Sylvian this morning."

"Who?"

"Sylvian de Beaune, the designer. I mentioned what we thought might have happened, and he went to check. The set's in store, you see, waiting for the definite go-ahead on the second pilot. Anyway, there it was—small polythene bag filled with sand, stuck on the back of the wheel with sticky tape, just opposite the crown. As you said."

"Quite a feat of improvisation, to sort that out in the studio."

"I think Mr Dyer went prepared."

"Took the sandbag with him, you mean?"

"Wouldn't surprise me. As we know, he's a *very dedicated* competitor. He knew the format of the show. He knew about the wheel. I think he planned it in advance."

"Bloody nerve. Where's the traditional British spirit of fair play?"

"That was invented before game shows."

"Yes. I suppose no one could have predicted the day when ritual humiliation would become a participant sport." Charles chuckled. "God, Tim would have been furious if he'd doctored the wheel and then someone else had got to the final."

"He was pretty confident it was going to be him. As he kept saying, there's a knack to these things. He knew what he was doing."

"Hmm. Presumably, if the show had run its course, he would have won his Austin Metro with no questions asked."

"Yes. Until you found out about his cheating, there was a possibility that he would have got it, anyway."

"Really?"

"Yes. All that guff I quoted from our Legal Department was sheer improvisation. I did consult them, but they were going to look for precedents and come back to me. So, you see, Charles, your quick thinking has saved W.E.T. a few thousand quid."

"Good. Not that I think W.E.T. needs the money, but I would really resent the idea of that little wimp Dyer getting it."

"I agree. Sylvian, incidentally, was furious."

"About what?"

"The idea of someone tampering with his set. It was his first big one, you see. He'd been assistant on a good few, but this was the first on which he was going to get a sole credit."

"I thought he looked rather nervous all day."

"He certainly did. Kept fiddling about and rearranging things. Anyway, he really blew his top when he saw what Tim had done. Said it ruined the game. He's got a strangely puritanical streak, Sylvian. He was particularly annoyed, because he'd already resisted one attempt to fix the result."

"What—another of the contestants tried it on?"

"No, no. It was John Mantle. He asked Sylvian to arrange that the wheel *didn't* end up with the crown on top."

"Good Lord."

"Well, it's an Executive Producer's job to keep his costs down. And it *was* only a pilot. Anyway, as I say, Sylvian refused to do it."

Charles was not given time to reflect on the perfidy of television producers as Sydnee went on, "So, where do we go next?"

"Which suspect, you mean?"

"Yes. We've still got Trish Osborne and Bob Garston—that is, assuming we've found out the full extent of Tim Dyer's evil-doing."

"I'm fairly confident we have. Well, of the other two suspects, Bob Garston at the moment seems much the more suspicious. Trish Osborne had very little opportunity to put the cyanide in the glass during the vital twenty minutes, whereas Bob was certainly around the studio area. He also stood to gain directly from Barrett's death. . . ."

"*Has* gained from it already. Heard this morning he's been definitely booked to host the second pilot."

"Has he? There was also that strange conversation Tim Dyer overheard . . ."

"About infidelity . . ."

"Yes, *marital* infidelity. . . . Could have meant that Bob's wife had been unfaithful. Has got a wife, has he?"

"Oh yes. She's an I.T.N. newscaster. I wonder who she was supposed to have been unfaithful with . . . ?"

"Be wonderfully neat if it turned out to be Barrett Doran. Which would also tie in with Bob's line about 'finding it difficult to work with the bastard under the circumstances'."

"Yes," Sydnee agreed excitedly. "And that would give Bob another reason for getting rid of his rival."

"All interesting speculation. Well, the person he was talking to, and who obviously knew what he was on about, was Joanie Bruton's husband. I think we should put Trish Osborne in cold storage for a while, and try and find out more from Roger Bruton."

"Probably mean talking to Joanie too. It's not often they're seen apart."

"That's fine. She may know even more about it. The

question is: How do we make the approach? Do you claim you want to talk about the second pilot? And, if so, how do you explain me away? Tim Dyer was too obsessed about his car to take much notice, but Joanie Bruton's no fool. I'm afraid she's likely to be rather more observant."

"Yes." There was a silence from the other end of the phone, while Sydnee made up her mind. "I think the best thing is to tell them the truth."

"Tell them that we don't think Chippy killed Barrett and we're trying to find out who did?" Charles asked, amazed.

"Yes. Why not? After all, they've both got rock-solid alibis for the relevant twenty minutes, so there's no way either of them could have been involved in the crime. Also, as you say, Joanie's a shrewd lady. I think she'd respect us more for telling her the truth. And we needn't worry about her discretion. By the nature of her work, she's used to keeping secrets."

"What about Roger?"

"He does what she does. No, the more I think about it, the more I'm convinced we should tell them everything. Joanie's a bright lady, and very understanding. I think she could help us a lot."

"Okay. If you're sure . . ."

"I am. Leave it to me, Charles. I'll set it up."

The house in Dulwich Village, outside which the MG drew up, was large, probably Edwardian. Its exterior had been recently decorated. A new Volvo was parked on the paved semicircle at the front.

The porch in which they stood as Sydnee pressed the bell-push was wooden-framed with the original windows of coloured glass. The red and white diamond tiles underfoot had been cleaned that morning.

Roger Bruton opened the door. Charles was again struck by his pallor which, combined with the wispy hair around his bald patch, gave him a slightly effete appearance. His voice, soft and precise, did nothing to dispel this impression.

"Good morning. You're right on time. I'm afraid Joanie hasn't quite finished her correspondence, but she'll be with us very shortly. Come through."

He led them across the tiled hallway and opened a stripped pine door into a large front room, which could be doubled in size when the folding partition doors were opened. A dumpy sofa and two dumpy armchairs gave a feeling of expensively casual comfort. A window-seat in the bay at the front was littered with apparently random cushions. Books were stacked with careful asymmetry on the shelves either side of the fireplace, in whose grate a Coalite fire glowed scarlet. Invitations and jocular cards were stuck into the frame of the high mirror above the mantelpiece. Everything demonstrated that perfection of cleanliness only to be found in a house without children.

"Do sit down, please." Roger gestured to the armchairs. Charles and Sydnee appropriated one each. They were both aware of a woman's voice talking rapidly and incisively on the other side of the partition.

Roger explained it immediately. "Joanie dictates her letters into a tape-recorder. Then her secretary comes in in the afternoon and types them up. It's the only way we can keep ahead. I'm afraid, what with the magazine and the radio spot and now the television show, the mail-bag just gets bigger every day."

"Actually," said Charles, "it was you we wanted to talk to, at least initially."

Roger Bruton looked startled at the suggestion. "I think it'd be better if you talked to both of us together. After all, I wasn't involved in the show at W.E.T., that was Joanie's bit. I was just sort of hanging around."

"Which must have given you an ideal chance to see what was going on."

"Oh, no. I'm not observant," said Roger Bruton, with a self-depreciating shrug, and then firmly changed the subject. He indicated a low table, on which stood a tray with a china coffee-set on it. Four cups and saucers were neatly laid out. "I'll just fill the pot. Coffee all right for both of you?"

They confirmed that it was, and he hurried out of the room with evident relief. "What did I tell you?" whispered Sydnee.

Charles might have responded to this, but the voice next door stopped, and they heard movement from behind the partition. The central door opened, and Joanie Bruton appeared. Charles rose to his feet.

"Good morning. Sorry to have kept you."

Seen close up, and in her own surroundings, she was strikingly pretty, tiny but perfectly proportioned. Her short hair was the kind of ash blond that melts almost imperceptibly into grey, she had a smooth, clear skin with only a tracery of lines around the eyes, and it was impossible to say what age she was. Anything from thirty to fifty. She was one of those fortunate women on whom time leaves little mark.

She briskly clattered the partition doors back, revealing a tidy office area at the other end of the room. On a red desk stood a word processor and two telephones. Colour-coded files filled one wall of shelves. It was all neatly expensive, like a home office design from a colour supplement.

She came and shook their hands. "Sorry, there wasn't a great deal of opportunity to get to know either of you on the studio day." She flopped gracefully on to the dumpy sofa and gestured Charles to sit, too. Turning her shrewd blue eyes on Sydnee, she said, "So you think the police have got the wrong murderer, love?"

"Yes. I'm convinced that Chippy didn't do it."

"Hmm. Is she a friend of yours?"

"Yes."

"It's quite natural that you should disbelieve it. We all get shocked when we hear unwelcome things about our friends. Apart from anything else, it seems to cast doubt on the quality of our own judgement. Pretending the unpalatable news is not true is quite a common reaction. Are you sure you're not just doing that, love?"

"Quite sure. We've almost got proof Chippy didn't do it."

Quickly, Charles explained about his drinking from Barrett Doran's glass at six-thirty. He slightly edited the truth, saying that he had just wanted to check the rumour going around that the host always had gin on the set, but Joanie's appraising eyes seemed to see through the subterfuge.

She looked pensive when he'd finished. "It never occurred to me to look for any other explanation of the death . . . I mean, once I'd heard the girl had been arrested. I suppose we can rule out the possibility of accident . . ."

"The cyanide had to be taken from Studio B, the gin had to be emptied out of the glass and the cyanide put in."

"No, you're right. It could hardly have been accidental. So that means you're looking for another murderer?"

At that moment Roger Bruton came into the room with the filled coffee-pot, and there was a pause while he filled the four cups and passed them round. When he was seated beside his wife on the sofa, she put her hand on his knee and said, "As I told you after the phone-call yesterday, Sydnee and Charles are convinced that the girl who's been arrested did not kill Barrett Doran."

"In that case," he asked almost without intonation, "what do they think happened?"

"Perhaps we should ask them," said Joanie. "Do you have any theories about what really went on?"

"Only vague theories," Charles replied. "I mean, obviously someone else murdered Barrett . . ."

The couple on the sofa seemed to relax slightly now this statement of the situation had been made.

". . . and we've been checking out the movements of people involved in the show during the relevant time."

"During the meal-break, you mean?" asked Roger.

"Well, only during a very specific part of it. The cyanide must have been put in the glass after six-thirty."

"After six-thirty?" Roger echoed in surprise.

"Yes, because I drank from Barrett's glass at six-thirty and it contained gin."

"Gin?" Another surprised echo.

"He always had gin when he was doing a show."

"Oh. And after you'd drunk from the glass, did you swap it round with one of the others?"

"No, of course he didn't," Joanie almost interrupted her husband. Then, more gently, she repeated, "No, of course he didn't, love." Turning to the others, she asked, "So . . . who are your suspects?"

Charles smiled. "Well, you'll be glad to hear that you two are off the list. You weren't down in the studio area at the pivotal time, so you're in the clear."

Joanie clutched at her throat in mock-panic. "What a relief."

"Just concentrating on the people who actually appeared on the show, we've ruled out all of the four 'professions'— that's except for me, assuming that I would be devious enough deliberately to stir up an investigation into my own guilt. . . ."

"I think we'll give you the benefit of the doubt."

"Very gracious. Of the four contestants, the only one who hasn't got an alibi for the relevant time—or perhaps I should say the only one whose alibi we haven't heard about—is the lady from Billericay, Trish Osborne. Of the panellists, you're all in the clear . . . except for Bob Garston."

"Ah." Joanie Bruton did not sound surprised, rather as if the mention of the name confirmed a suspicion.

"Now, at the moment we are concentrating our investigations on Bob Garston. As I say, he had the opportunity, and he had at least some motive."

"Oh?" Charles got the impression that Joanie knew something, but was biding her time, waiting to see how much of it they knew already.

"He was considered for the job of hosting *If The Cap Fits*," Sydnee explained. "In fact, he's going to do it on the second pilot."

"So you reckon that was the reason he would want Barrett out of the way?"

Again Charles felt Joanie was holding back, unwilling to volunteer more than she had to.

"That's one reason. We've a feeling there may also have been something more personal."

She raised a quizzical eyebrow at him. "Like what?"

"That's why we've come to see you. We thought you might know something about his private life."

She chuckled. "I know a great deal about a great many people's private lives, love. But one of the reasons why people tell me things, and the reason why I keep my job, is because I respect the confidentiality of such secrets."

"Of course."

While Charles tried to think of the next move, Sydnee came in, typically direct. "You were overheard, Roger, talking to Bob. There was a suggestion that Bob Garston's wife had been having an affair with someone."

This shook Roger Bruton. "Who overheard me? Who was spying on me? Where were they? What did they see?"

Again his wife's calming hand went on to his knee. "It's all right, love, all right." She turned her eyes on Charles. "Since you seem to know already, I can't do any harm by confirming it. Yes. Bob's wife did have an affair."

"With Barrett Doran?"

She nodded. "I knew about it, because I was there when they met. On some Thames Television chat-show. I saw them go off together. It was obvious to me what was happening. I do know a bit about the mechanics of sexual attraction."

"Was Bob around at the time?"

"No. He heard about it, though. His wife must have told him herself, because nobody else knew. I gather he took it pretty badly. I talked to him about it when we next met, told him that these things happen, that often a little fling like that needn't affect the basic stability of the marriage." She had dropped into the no-nonsense counselling manner she used to telephone callers on her weekly radio programme.

"And it wasn't in the gossip columns or anything? I had understood Barrett liked to make his conquests public."

"Not this one. I think she must've insisted on keeping it quiet. I never heard it even hinted at by anyone."

"Was the affair still going on when Barrett died?"

"No. Only lasted about a month, I think. Bob and she didn't split up or anything. I gather they'd more or less got over it, but Bob must have found it difficult suddenly having to be in the same studio as the man who'd cuckolded him."

"How difficult, I wonder?"

"What you mean is, did it make Bob angry enough to decide to kill his rival? Who can say? People react differently to things. With some the trigger to violence is very delicately balanced; others will put up with almost anything."

"And what would your professional judgement be of Bob Garston in that respect?"

"Do I see him as a potential murderer?"

"Yes."

"On balance, no. I can see him getting very angry, and I can see him contemplating violence against someone who he reckoned had wronged him. But I think that violence would be expressed much more openly. I can see him going up to Barrett and punching him on the nose, but this devious business with the cyanide . . . no, doesn't sound his style."

"I think you're probably barking up the wrong tree," said Roger Bruton abruptly. "The police aren't fools. They don't arrest people without good reason. I'm sure the girl they've got is the right one."

"Yes, Roger," his wife agreed soothingly, "but you can see why Charles and Sydnee want to try and prove otherwise. It would be terrible if the wrong person did get sentenced for the crime."

Roger Bruton did not look as if he agreed, but he didn't pursue the argument further.

"I know we're just feeling our way at the moment," Charles admitted, "but we do definitely think that we're on to something."

"Of course." Joanie's voice was very nearly patronizing as she said the line that had become her catch-phrase. "I fully understand, love."

"Tell me, as someone who was in the studio all through the show, did you notice anything strange at any point?"

"Strange?"

"Did anyone appear to be behaving oddly, anyone on the panel, any of the contestants . . . ?"

"Well, no one was behaving very naturally, but then it's hardly a very natural situation. Everyone was tense, of course, concentrating on their performance. Is that what you mean?"

"No, I meant more than that. Did you notice anyone doing anything that you thought at the time was out of character?"

"I don't think so, love, no."

"And, when Barrett drank the poison, did you notice anyone reacting in an unusual way?"

"Good heavens." She chuckled. "You ask a lot. It was a moment of terrible shock when he started gasping. We were none of us in any state to start checking each other's reactions. We just all leapt up to see if we could do anything to help him."

A new thought came into Charles's mind. "The desk got knocked over when you all stood up."

"Yes. That big oaf, Nick Jeffries. There's a lot of him, you know. The original bull in the china shop."

"Hmm. Yes." Charles looked across at Sydnee. "I think that really covers everything we were going to ask, doesn't it?"

The researcher nodded.

"We're very grateful to you both for giving up your time. As I say, we are still just feeling around. And I know we've voiced suspicions which are almost certainly scandalous. . . ."

"My mind," said Joanie, "is the repository of so much scandal that the odd bit more's not going to hurt. It's as safe as a numbered Swiss bank account. Lots and lots of secrets locked away in there, aren't there, love?"

She grinned at her husband, who gave a nervous grin back.

"So where do you go from here?" he asked Charles.

"With our investigations?"

"Yes. If you persist in thinking there's anything to investigate," he added sceptically.

"Well, I suppose we try and find out more about Bob Garston's movements during the meal-break. You saw him. Were you with him for long?"

"No. I'd just left Joanie in Make-up and I met him outside. We walked along the corridor and parted at the lifts."

"Did he get into a lift?"

"Yes, he did."

"Didn't say where he was going?"

"No."

"And you stayed down waiting for Joanie?"

"Yes. There's a sort of Reception area there with chairs. I sat and waited."

"I don't suppose you saw anything odd going on round the studios?"

"I wondered when you were going to ask me that," Roger Bruton announced primly. "Yes, I did see something rather odd going on."

"What?" asked Charles.

Joanie Bruton said nothing, but she looked hard at her husband. Her expression was one of surprise mixed with something that could have been alarm.

Roger Bruton relished his moment centre stage. "I saw the Trish Osborne person. Looking most unhappy. Crying, in fact."

"What was she doing?"

He smiled smugly. "Coming out of Barrett Doran's dressing room."

Chapter Nine

"FRANCES. IT'S ME, Charles."

"Keeping rather earlier hours than usual." Her voice was unruffled, warm without being positively welcoming. If she was surprised to hear from him after three months, she didn't show it.

"I wanted to catch you before you went to school."

"Well, you have. Just. I have to be in the car in three minutes."

He visualized her yellow Renault 5 parked outside the house, then remembered he was projecting the wrong image. She had moved out of the Muswell Hill home they had shared and now lived in a flat in Highgate. He had not been there often enough to visualize the Renault 5 outside it.

"Listen, I wondered if we could meet up . . ."

"Another reconciliation?" Her voice was wary.

"Just to see you. I just want to see you."

"Well . . ."

"Couldn't we meet for dinner tonight? Not at the flat. That Italian place in Hampstead. What do you say?"

"Well . . ."

"Come on. I'll behave myself. No romantic red roses. No unwelcome attentions . . . that is, if they really are unwelcome. . . ."

"Watch it. You're on the verge of the 'women always mean yes when they say no' heresy."

"No, I didn't mean that. I'd just like to see you, talk about things . . ." Then with inspiration he added, ". . . talk about Juliet, talk about our grandchildren . . ."

"Charles, I had just reconciled myself to the idea that I wasn't going to hear from you again for a long time."

"Well, unreconcile yourself."

"I'm not sure. You've no idea, once the initial hurt and emptiness had worn off, just how restful the thought of not seeing you for a while has become."

"Oh."

She responded to the disappointment in his monosyllable by asking cautiously, "You don't just want to see me because you're depressed, do you? Because I'm pretty ragged by this stage in the term, and I don't think I've much spare capacity for the old hand-holding 'I understand, I understand' routine."

"I'm not depressed. Not more than usual."

"Great," she said with resignation. "Have you just come to the end of one of your little affairs?"

"No. Honestly. There hasn't been anyone on the scene for months . . . nearly a year."

"Hmm."

"Oh, come on, Frances, do have dinner with me. After all, I am your husband."

As soon as he'd said it, he knew that this might not be the best argument to put forward, and it received a well-deserved slap-down. "Depends very much, I would have said, on your definition of 'husband' . . . whether the word is a once-and-for-all title bestowed at marriage or whether it implies a continuing active role, like, say, the word 'lover'."

"I don't quite see what you're getting at," he said evasively.

"Yes, you do. The word 'lover' suggests something's happening. When the affair's over, people become 'ex-lovers'. It's not the same with 'husband'. Even if the marriage is over, you don't become an 'ex-husband' without getting divorced."

"Oh, you're not on about that again. I thought we agreed that there was no point in our getting divorced."

"*You* agreed that. I don't recall my opinion being canvassed."

"Frances . . ."

"I have to be in the car in twenty seconds."

"Frances, will you please meet me for dinner in the Italian place at eight o'clock this evening?"

"All right. But, Charles Paris . . ."

"Yes?"

"Don't you dare be late."

"I won't be, love. You know me."

"Yes. I do."

Sydnee had said she'd ring him once she'd fixed up for them to see Trish Osborne, and she came through about half-past ten.

"She's set up. Happy to talk. I said we'd be over early afternoon."

"Did you say what we wanted to talk about?"

"No. Mind you, she didn't ask. Presumably, like Tim Dyer, she just assumes it's something to do with the show."

"Good. Well, look, can you pick me up at the bedsitter? Or will it be easier if I make my way to somewhere more central . . . ?"

"Charles, I've got problems here. Just after I'd spoken to Trish, John Mantle came in. I'm afraid I've got to start out on the contestant trail again."

"For the second pilot?"

"Yes. They've got a studio date now. The schedule's been rejigged so that the pilot goes into Studio A next Thursday. Which means we've got to get a move on getting the contestants."

114

"I thought you always had some spares lined up."

"Yes, but I don't think they'd be good enough for John. The American copyright-holders have been bending his ear. They say the contestants we had on the first pilot showed about as much life as General Custer after Little Big Horn. They say we've got to get a new lot with more 'pazazz'."

"Where do you start looking for 'pazazz'?"

"Same places as I looked when 'pazazz' wasn't on the shopping-list. The trouble is, what these Americans don't realize is that people over here haven't yet lost their inhibitions about game shows. It's going to take a few years before the British reserve cracks and you see the kind of hysterical commitment you get in the States. Still, from John Mantle's point of view, I must be seen to be busy. Four brand-new contestants with 'pazazz' must be found."

"Are the contestants the only changes you'll make in casting?"

"Well, obviously we'll need one new celeb now Bob's moved up to host. Lots of names have been mentioned, but I don't think it's been offered to anyone yet. And we'll have to set up four more 'professions'."

"Oh." Charles saw a potential booking disappearing over the horizon.

"Come on, Charles, we couldn't book you lot again. With three of the same celebs on the panel, they're going to remember what your real professions were."

"I doubt it. They didn't take any notice of us, didn't see us as people at all. I bet, if I was back on, two of them'd still think I was the hamburger chef."

"You're probably right. But we can't take the risk. People get very uptight about these game shows. Any hint of rigging or cheating or someone being 'in the know', and you can get some very nasty reactions."

"I suppose so."

"Anyway, Chita's busy setting up four new 'professions'—'professions', of course, who might just conceivably wear hats, which let me tell you, is not as easy as it sounds— and I have got to shoot off to Manchester to interview some punters in the fruitless search for 'pazazz'."

"Oh."

"What I'm saying, Charles, is can you go and interview Trish Osborne on your own?"

"But what ever excuse can I give for being there? At least, with you, I'd have some sort of W.E.T. credibility, but on my own . . ."

"I'm sure you'll think of something, Charles."

It took Charles longer than he had expected to get to Billericay, and it was after four when he finally reached the neat dark-red-brick three-bedroomed house where Trish Osborne lived.

He got a whiff of perfume as she opened the door, and saw that she was wearing a pale-blue flying-suit. She had dressed up for her continuing contact with the media world.

Though he had had plenty of travelling time during which to work out his excuse for appearing on her doorstep, he hadn't come up with much. "I'm afraid Sydnee suddenly had to go to Manchester," he said lamely, "so there's just me."

"Never mind." She ushered him into her living-room. The carpet had a yellow and green zigzag design, whose colours were picked up on the open curtains. White patterned net against the double glazing shut out the darkening world. The mahogany veneer surface of the dining table gleamed, as did the yellow-upholstered chairs marshalled around it. Light refracted through the spotless glass ornaments above the matt silver music centre on the room-divider. On the walls, in yellow velvet tasselled frames, were photographs of three children at different ages. In pride of place, on the mantelpiece over the "log-effect" gas fire, lay her red, blue and silver *If The Cap Fits* cap.

She gestured to a lime-green three-piece suite with dark wood arm-rests and rigidly plumped yellow cushions. "Do sit down. What can I get you? Tea? Coffee? Something stronger?"

This last was offered with a kind of insouciant daring, Trish demonstrating her freedom from the conventional restraints which might have inhibited someone not accustomed to media circles.

Charles resisted the temptation. "Tea'd be lovely."

She must have had the kettle boiling when he arrived, because she appeared in only a couple of minutes with a loaded tray. Charles still hadn't worked out his line of approach, so, while she poured, he played for time by indicating the photographs. "Nice-looking kids."

"Yes. Taken some time ago. They're all grown-up now."

"Really?"

"Youngest's twenty."

He looked at her. He knew it was going to be a corny line, but it was still true. "You don't look old enough to have children of that age."

She coloured very slightly in acknowledgement of the compliment. Her dark hair was even shorter, must have been cut since the recording. It came down to little peaks in front of her small ears. "If you start breeding at seventeen, it's quite possible to have them all off your hands by the time you're forty." She hesitated. "And then look around to see if there's anything left of your life."

"Lots, I'm sure." Charles smiled in meaningless reassurance. "Even at my age, one still hopes there are more good bits to come."

She didn't look convinced. Nor did she look at ease, perched on the edge of her lime-green armchair. Charles took a long swallow of tea. He still hadn't decided how to explain his presence. True, she hadn't questioned it yet, but the moment must come.

He made a kind of start. "Terrible business at the recording, wasn't it?"

"Yes. The poor girl. I mean, I know men can be bastards, but to be driven to that . . . to kill someone . . ."

"Yes. Poor Chippy."

"I thought the name was Caroline something."

"Chippy was her nickname, the name she used at work."

"I wonder what she'll get. Surely not life for something like that . . . ? I mean it was a crime of passion, wasn't it?"

"I suppose so. Though that's not always a category the British Law recognizes. She could still get a hefty sentence."

"But I'd have thought when something's spur-of-the-moment like that . . ."

"Not completely spur-of-the-moment. Taking the cyanide from one studio to the other must have involved a degree of premeditation."

"As I said, poor girl . . ."

Charles decided to take a risk. "There has been talk around W.E.T. that maybe she wasn't the one who did it. . . ."

"What do you mean?"

"There have been suggestions that someone else killed Barrett Doran."

"What!" She turned her wide brown eyes on him in amazement. Either the idea was a total shock to her, or she was putting up a very skilful front. Charles, who knew a bit about the subject, didn't think she was a good enough actress to be shamming. He decided it was worth taking another risk. The truth, he had often found, could be a useful surprise tactic.

"In fact, that's why I'm here. As I say, various people at W.E.T. have had doubts about Chippy's guilt and I'm just sort of investigating, on their behalf, to see if there's any other possible explanation for what happened."

"I see." The eyes went down quickly, but not quickly

enough to hide their disappointment. "And, if Sydnee had been able to come today, is that what she would have been coming about?"

"Yes."

"Ah." The hurt was still there.

"Why, what did you imagine she might—?"

"Nothing, nothing."

Charles looked at the bowed dark head in its neat suburban living-room, and suddenly he saw everything. It was just another manifestation of the power of television. Trish Osborne thought she had done well on *If The Cap Fits*. And indeed she had. She had been a good lively contestant (in spite of what Aaron Greenberg and Dirk van Henke felt). But that was all she had been. She, with that ignorance of scale that always afflicts amateurs, had not recognized the limits of her performance. She had seen it as the start of something. With time on her hands at home for ideas to grow like ginger-beer plants, she had fantasized of directors hailing her as a "natural" for television, of offers of work, of a new impetus to dig her out of her domestic rut, of a career to fill the void left by her departed children. She had thought that Sydnee's wish to see her would be about the next step on that ladder. It was all very commonplace, very predictable and very sad.

He knew he was right, but he passed no comment on his findings. "So I'm here, really, to ask you to think back over that studio day, think if there was anything suspicious, anything you noticed that seemed out of the ordinary."

She laughed, jogging herself out of self-pity. "The whole day seemed pretty out of the ordinary to me. I'd never been in a television studio before. It may seem pretty ordinary to you, but let me tell you, being on television is the answer to many a Billericay housewife's dreams." Her face clouded. "I suppose, after what happened, I'm not even going to *be* on television. I mean, there's no way they can put out that recording, is there?"

"No."

She clutched at a straw. "They couldn't sort of edit on another ending . . . ?

Charles shook his head. "Sorry, love." (For a moment he wondered, "Do I normally say 'love' as much as this, or have I picked it up from the infinitely understanding Joanie Bruton?") "Think about it—with a show of that sort, you can't suddenly change hosts in the middle. You couldn't even if there had been no publicity about Barrett's death. As it is . . ."

"Yes, I'm sorry. I was just being silly. Not thinking. Of course they couldn't use it."

Moved again by the disappointment in her eyes, Charles searched for another reassurance. "It probably hasn't made that much difference, actually, love." (Doing it again.) "With a show like this, they'd be very unlikely to put out the pilot. They'd be almost bound to want to make some changes in the casting or the format before they got into a series."

This was not at all the right thing to say. The brown eyes blazed. "What, you mean we went through all that for nothing? We were just being used as guinea pigs with no chance of the show actually being on the television? The producer swore it would go out unless there was something terribly wrong."

"Well," said Charles, redirecting the conversation off this sticky patch, "there was something terribly wrong, wasn't there?"

This brought her up short. "Yes," she replied softly.

"Barrett Doran's death. Can we talk about that?"

"If you like." She remained subdued, still inwardly boiling at the perfidy of a television company that could put her under such strain on what she regarded as false pretences.

"Starting from the idea that Chippy didn't kill her former lover . . ."

"Was he? I didn't know that."

"Yes. That was presumed to be her motive. 'Hell hath no fury . . .'"

"Sorry?"

"'. . . like a woman scorned.'"

She gave a small shake of her head. The quotation didn't mean anything to her.

"Anyway, if Chippy didn't, somebody else did. And the murderer put cyanide in Barrett Doran's drink at a very specific time. During the meal-break, between six-thirty and ten to seven. Sydnee and I have been going round, checking up on the movements of people connected with the show at that time."

"Oh yes?" There was a new reticence in her manner; she didn't volunteer anything.

"I wondered what you were doing then, Trish . . . ?"

She coloured. "Oh, you know. This and that. I can't really remember."

"You left Chita in the Conference Room at a quarter past six. You were back in there at twenty to seven. You left the room with Tim Dyer. You both said you fancied a steak. Neither of you had one."

"You *have* been doing your research."

"Outside the Conference Room you both got into separate lifts. I want to know what you did for the next twenty-five minutes."

She now looked very flustered. "I said. I can't really remember. I was very nervous. I just walked about to calm me down."

"This is important, Trish. I'm talking about the time that the cyanide was put into the glass."

The brown eyes widened. "But surely you don't think that *I* had anything to do with it?"

"I'm just trying to eliminate as many people as possible from suspicion," Charles replied stolidly, in a voice he'd used as a Detective-Inspector in an Agatha Christie play ("About as lively as a Yorkshire pudding that's still wet in the middle"—*West Sussex Gazette*).

"Well, there wasn't anything suspicious about what I was doing."

"Trish," he said with a little more force, "nothing was seen of you from the moment you got into the lift . . . until you came out of Barrett Doran's dressing room at about twenty-five past six. At which time you were crying."

She looked for a second as if she might be about to cry again, but then regained control of herself and appeared to make the decision to tell the truth. "All right. I did go to his dressing room."

"Straight after you came out of the lift in the basement?"

"Yes."

"Why did you go there?"

"He'd invited me for a drink." The words were dragged out truculently.

"And you agreed to have a drink with him? Even after the way he had humiliated you in the afternoon?"

Her blush spread down her neck. Charles's eyes, unwillingly following it, were uncomfortably aware, through the thin material of the flying-suit, of the unmentioned subject of their conversation.

"Yes, I suppose he had humiliated me. But I overreacted. I shouldn't have burst into tears on the set. I know you've got to be tough if you're going to get anywhere in television." She repeated this last line devoutly, like an article of faith.

"Presumably, when you agreed to go and have a drink with him, you were aware of Barrett Doran's reputation as a womanizer?"

"That's why I agreed," she almost snapped at him. Charles gaped. "God, have you any idea how boring life is in

Billericay? I want my life to *start*, I want to catch up on all the things I missed while I was having babies and polishing furniture. No, I didn't like Barrett Doran, he'd upset me a lot during the rehearsal, but I knew that he fancied me. I wasn't going to miss a chance. I know you have to sleep around if you're going to get anywhere in television."

This again was spoken like part of a creed, received wisdom which she had picked up and was determined to believe. Charles found himself shocked by her strange mixture of outrageousness and naïveté, and a little frightened by the desperation that accompanied it.

"So can I enquire what happened when you got into his dressing room?"

"Don't see why not." Her attempt at brazen insouciance was not coming off. There was something engagingly pathetic about it, like a teenager adding a couple of years to her age at a party. "Fairly predictable, really. He poured me a drink, then he put his arms round me and started to kiss me. That was what I had expected, so it wasn't such a big deal. . . ."

"But. . . ." Charles voiced the unspoken conjunction.

"*But* he was a bit too . . . He rushed me. I wasn't quite ready for . . . I hadn't expected him to . . ." All the skin above her neckline was now deep red. ". . . to want to do it so quickly," she pronounced finally.

"He hadn't got long. Only time for a quickie," said Charles without much emphasis.

"Anyway, he was scrabbling at my clothes, trying to undress me—not all of me, just the bits he needed, and I was sort of holding him back, but not quite holding him back and . . . and then the door opened."

She sat back in her chair, relieved, as if the worst part of the narrative was over.

"It was a girl. Blonde girl. Pretty, I suppose. I didn't recognize her."

123

"Had she got on a light-grey sort of all-in-one suit . . . cut like the one you're wearing?" Trish nodded. "That was Chippy, the one who's been charged with his murder."

"Good heavens. Was it? I didn't really look at her. You know, I was flustered, pulling my clothes around me. It was . . . well, it was embarrassing."

"And was that what made you cry?"

"No. It was what Barrett said to me." She looked once again tearful at the recollection.

"Can I ask . . . ?"

"I won't tell you exactly what he said, but he dismissed me, as if I were . . . I don't know, a waiter, a taxi-driver . . . no one . . . as if I wasn't a person at all."

"I'm rather afraid that's how he treated most people."

"Yes." She seemed listless, tired out by her account.

"So you left the dressing room and went out into the corridor?"

"Yes."

"Where you met Roger Bruton."

"I saw him. I turned away. I didn't want him to see I was crying."

"Any particular reason, or wouldn't you have wanted anyone to see you crying?"

"I wouldn't want anyone to, but . . ." She let out a little cough of laughter ". . . I particularly didn't want him to. I was afraid he'd get Joanie to come along and ask what the matter was. I couldn't have faced her *understanding* me. God knows how he's stuck it all these years. What hell it must be for a man whose wife really *understands* him."

"Most men complain of the opposite."

"Do you?" Her brown eyes found his.

"Complain that my wife doesn't understand me? No, I'm rather afraid she does. But, since we've been separated for fifteen years or so, the point's really academic." He needed to break the link between their eyes, so he looked away and moved briskly on. "You left Barrett's dressing room at about twenty-five past six. You weren't back up in the Conference Room till twenty to seven."

"No."

"What did you do? Can you account for that quarter of an hour?"

"I went to the Ladies, the one near Make-up. I was crying. I didn't want people to see me crying. I went to sort of pull myself together."

It was a fairly shaky alibi, but she said it so ingenuously Charles felt inclined to believe her. "Did you see anyone apart from Roger Bruton before you got back to the Conference Room?"

"I saw Bob Garston."

"Oh?"

"After I'd come out of the Ladies. While I was waiting for the lift. It took ages to come. Bob came and waited too."

"Did he say anything?"

"Commented on how inefficient the lifts were, that sort of thing. I was still trying to hide the fact that I'd been crying, so I didn't want to make conversation."

"No. And this'd be . . . what? Round twenty to seven?"

"Must've been by then, yes."

"And when the lift finally came, did you both travel up to the fifth floor together?"

She nodded.

"I don't suppose you saw where Bob came from? Did he walk all the way along the corridor to the lifts?"

"Oh no. He came out of one of the doors half-way along."

"Do you remember which one?"

"Yes, certainly. The door from Studio A."

"Ah," said Charles, as non-committally as he could, smothering the surge of excitement inside him.

Trish Osborne did not seem aware of the portent of her words. She stretched her arms behind her neck and yawned.

The movement emphasized what Barrett Doran had thought unsuitable for family viewing. "That's really tired me out, going through all that again. Let's have a real drink now."

Charles didn't refuse, and was soon equipped with a large glass of Chivas Regal. Trish had a schooner of sherry. She sat down on the sofa beside him and looked at her watch. "That's not bad. Kept off the booze till half-past five today."

This remark, like some of her earlier ones, seemed designed only to shock. Charles did not react. He reckoned he had got what he came for. Bob Garston had been seen coming out of Studio A at exactly the right time. The investigation was proceeding.

"Nothing else you can remember struck you as odd during the studio day? Nothing that happened just before his actual death or . . . ?"

"I wouldn't have seen it if there had been anything. I was eliminated, remember."

"Oh yes, of course. Well, did your husband see anything from the audience?"

She let out a short, bitter laugh. "He wasn't there. He's not interested in any of my activities."

"Oh."

"The only thing that interests him is his work. That's why he gets home at ten every night. 'Working late at the office.' Classic cover-up for an affair. I sometimes think I wouldn't mind if it *was* an affair. At least that'd give another dimension to him, he wouldn't be one hundred per cent boring. But I'm afraid, in his case, no, it really *is* work."

"Oh," said Charles. Trish seemed closer to him now on the sofa, her shoulder brushing against his. He sat forward. "Really should be off. I'm very grateful to you for . . ."

"There's no hurry. Have another drink."

"Oh no, I shouldn't, well, just a small one."

It wasn't a small one. Trish's refill wasn't small, either. She suddenly giggled as she bounced down on to the sofa

126

beside him. "Awfully embarrassing, wasn't it, in the studio, that business about my blouse? I bet you didn't know where to look."

"Oh, it was . . . all right. I'm sure you were more embarrassed than anyone else was. I've seen that sort of thing happen a lot before."

"Oh?" She arched an eyebrow.

"Well, I mean, I've been to lots of costume calls and photo calls where that kind of thing arises—I mean, happens." He didn't think he was doing this very well. "There are always problems like that. Men have to be told to put jock-straps under their tights and ladies . . . well. . . ." He found his eyes were ineluctably drawn to the objects of discussion. "Happens all the time in the theatre," he babbled. "Always has. Dr Johnson told David Garrick he'd have to stop going backstage because the actresses' breasts unsettled him."

Trish Osborne did not seem over-interested in this snippet of literary anecdote. Instead, she looked down at her cleavage. "Barrett Doran was wrong, actually."

"Oh. What about?"

"Well, he said they'd gone like that because I was panting for it."

"Oh yes, so he did. I remember vaguely."

"That wasn't the reason. It was just nerves, you know, being in the studio and all that."

"Oh. Well, there you go."

"I mean, the effect is the same, but it *was* nerves."

"Ah."

"It's not nerves now," she said.

Charles felt bad as he entered the restaurant in Hampstead. In spite of her apparent sophistication, it turned out that he was the first man with whom Trish had cheated on her husband, and that had led to a few tears. Also the brazenness of her approach, and the fact that he was clearly not an individual but some rite of passage into her fifth decade, left him feeling soiled.

And he was late. Twenty to nine.

There was no softness in Frances's face as she demanded, "Where the hell have you been?"

"Oh," he said. "Billericay."

Chapter Ten

BOB GARSTON'S CAREER was on an upward spiral. His early success as an on-screen researcher for a pop consumer programme had given him public recognition. People stopped him in the streets, turned their heads as he passed, pointed to him in restaurants. He loved all the attention.

And he got more of it when he started his own series. A shrewd producer, recognizing how readily people identified with Bob Garston, had devised a format which used his populist qualities to the full. The show was called *Joe Soap* and its piously avowed intention was to explain the workings of bureaucracy to the general public. Each week Bob Garston in his *faux-naïf* role as Joe Soap would attempt some enterprise—to have a house extension built, to take the Gas Board to court, to set up his own minicab business—and go through the necessary bureaucratic hoops to realize that ambition.

His interviews with the various officials were filmed, and these film inserts linked in the studio by Bob, whose wry commentary was interspersed with recollections and horror stories from "ordinary people" who had been through the same processes. As ever in television programmes dealing with members of the public, their contribution was edited with professional cunning to extract the maximum humour and, almost always, to leave them looking stupid.

The series was an instant success. Its format skilfully provided the audience with a justification for laughing at their fellow human beings. Like an investigative television sex programme, and with the same degree of calculation on the part of its makers, *Joe Soap* was watched by most of its viewers for the wrong reasons.

The series, like the earlier consumer programme, was made by the B.B.C. Bob Garston's only work for I.T.V. had hitherto been a few guest appearances on quiz show panels. His assumption of Barrett Doran's mantle on *If The Cap Fits* would be an important stepping-stone towards the big money and wider audience of commercial television.

These thoughts went through Charles Paris's head as he sat with Sydnee watching the recording of the latest *Joe Soap*. She had had a legitimate excuse for contacting Bob Garston, since John Mantle had delegated her to check through the format of *If The Cap Fits* with its new host. Long circular harangues from Aaron Greenberg and Dirk van Henke had led the Executive Producer to make a few revisions in the proposed presentation of the show. Patience and his customary diplomacy had ensured that these changes were minimal and cosmetic, but he had given straight-faced assurances to the copyright-holders that every detail would be communicated to the new host.

(The Americans had not been convinced that Bob Garston was the right man for the job. They saw little evidence that he possessed the "pazazz" which, to their minds, Barrett Doran had lacked. Once again, John Mantle had had to spend many hours of cajoling and apparent concession over expensive food before he got his own way. At least one good thing had emerged out of the first pilot, however; the Americans had been so concerned about other details that they put up no further objections to the English title for the show. On that point, John Mantle's slow, wait-and-see diplomacy had paid off, and he felt confident that, given time and patience, it would pay off on the other details too.)

Though Sydnee had a perfectly legitimate reason for going to see Bob Garston, explaining Charles's presence at the recording was going to be more difficult. Bob had suggested a meal after the show to Sydnee, secure in the glamour of his television persona (and not realizing that her long exposure to the medium had left her a little more cynical than most women about that glamour). Charles had, needless to say, not been included in the invitation, and he had a feeling his being there would cast him in the unwelcome role of gooseberry. Whether or not Bob Garston had sexual designs on Sydnee, he was the kind of man whose ego would be massaged by dining alone with any attractive girl.

On the other hand, the way their investigation into Barrett Doran's death was pointing made both determined that they should confront their suspect together.

Sydnee reckoned their best approach would be an edited version of the truth. They should voice their suspicions that Chippy had not killed Stacey and say that they were trying desperately to clear her. For that reason, they were talking to all those who had been involved in the show, trying to find out if anyone had seen anything that might help their case. They would not make any direct accusation to Bob, but hope that something he said might confirm their suspicions.

Charles thought this was pretty risky. If Bob Garston were guilty, it would only alert him to his danger and lead him into evasion. But, try as he could, Charles couldn't come up with another, safer approach, so he had been forced to accept Sydnee's suggestion, unsatisfactory though it was.

He sat back and watched the show. Bob Garston, with the mock-innocence of Joe Soap, was on film, applying to a Local Council Planner for permission to build a greenhouse in his back garden. "But suppose I just put the thing up, I'm sure you wouldn't really mind. . . . You'd turn a blind eye. . . . Don't you think?"

"Oh, I couldn't do that."

Charles, who knew a lot about vocal inflections, could recognize that the Planner had been going to say more, but had been cut short by the edit. The effect was exactly as the programme-makers intended. The man sounded as if the thing he "couldn't do" was "to think". The audience duly roared their approval of this ambiguity.

Cut back to Bob Garston in the studio. "Well," he said with a wolfish grin, rubbing in the joke for those too slow to understand first time round, "he said it!"

The audience around Charles again roared sycophantically.

Getting "a television person" on his own is never easy. Programme-making always involves a lot of people and those who work in the medium tend to hunt in packs. To see a single person, or even just a couple, in a television bar is a rarity; instead there are clusters, large groups representing different production teams.

There was a large *Joe Soap* group round Bob Garston in the B.B.C. Television Centre bar that evening after the recording. Sydnee and Charles were the exception, just two people, drinking respectively white wine and Bell's whisky. Bob had waved recognition at Sydnee through the crowd in his dressing room, led her up with the crowd to the bar, and joined the crowd at the entrance to sign her in. Charles had taken advantage of the crowd to sidle in without benefit of signature. Bob had shown no sign of recognizing him. The problem of explaining his presence remained.

Beyond buying her a drink, Bob Garston had made no attempt to include Sydnee in his group. As a television person, she understood this completely. She knew the wild laughter and gesticulation around him was part of that mutual release of tension that came at the end of a long studio day. She knew that all the conversation would be of late cues, shadows from microphone booms, recalcitrant interviewees, references and in-jokes that could have no meaning for those who had not lived through the same day.

Charles had no expectation of being included. His dominant worry remained how to explain himself, how to make sure that he and Sydnee got a chance to talk to Bob alone. He looked around the bar, and saw a couple of actors he knew buying drinks for Light Entertainment producers. He felt the recurrent wave of despair that came over him whenever he thought about his career. He knew actors should keep a high profile, be seen by the people who mattered, the people who controlled that arcane magic of employment. On the rare occasions when his agent ceased to think of him as a lost cause and proffered advice, Maurice Skellern always said, "Put yourself about, Charles, get yourself seen. Got to be up front as an actor, you know. Remind people you exist. Actors got to let their light be seen, shine upon producers, dazzle them. Whereas all you seem to do is find thicker and thicker bushels to hide yours under."

He knew partly it was true. Some of his failure in his chosen career could be attributed to the eternal problem of too many actors chasing too few parts, some perhaps to only an average talent, but within him there was also the fatal flaw of diffidence, a kind of laziness that kept him from hustling as hard as he knew he should.

Sounds of an argument at the bar shook him out of this orbit of self-pity. Time had been called, but one of the Light Entertainment producers was vigorously asserting that he needed another drink. People were starting to look around for abandoned handbags and briefcases. The party was breaking up.

With many good-humoured waves and shoulder-slappings, Bob Garston detached himself from the *Joe Soap* group and came across towards them. "Sydnee, hi. You set?"

"Sure." She indicated her companion. "This is Charles Paris."

"Oh yes?" There was no interest and no recognition in his glance.

"You remember, he was one of the 'professions' in the first *If The Cap Fits* pilot."

Bob gave a nod which recognized this fact without giving it any importance. With a perfunctory grin at Charles, he reached out an arm to Sydnee. "Shall we be off then?"

She looked at Charles with an expression that told him he had to get out of this one. "Bob," he said. "We want to talk to you."

"Sydnee and I are just going off to talk. I don't see where you fit in."

"We want to talk about Barrett Doran's murder."

Bob Garston's eyes narrowed. The hearty public face slipped away, to be replaced by something more furtive.

"You'd better come along then," he said.

Bob Garston's car was directly in front of Television Centre, where only the highly privileged were allowed to park. It was a new Jaguar. Bob and Charles sat in the front, Sydnee in the back.

"Right, what is this?" The voice was unrecognizable from the confident, insinuating tones of Joe Soap. It was breathier, tighter; and the note of tension could have been fear.

Charles explained evenly, without specifying their reasons, that they didn't think Chippy had killed Barrett.

"And are you going to make your suspicions public? Are you going to the police?"

"We will eventually, yes. We'd rather go with the name of the person who did kill him and some evidence to prove it. But if we can't get that fairly soon, we'll just have to go and tell them why we know Chippy's innocent."

"Why is that?"

"We have our reasons," Charles replied infuriatingly.

Bob Garston was silent for a moment. Then he said, "You realize that, if the girl's eliminated, I become the obvious suspect?"

This was too easy. "Yes," said Charles. "That's the conclusion we were coming to."

"I wanted the host job from the start. I never made much secret of the fact. I don't believe in disguising ambition. I think if you say what you want, you stand a damned sight better chance of getting it." The forthright Joe Soap quality came back briefly into his voice. "So I suppose that could look like a motive . . ."

"Not the only one," said Charles gently.

A light that had not been switched off in an office above them filtered through the windscreen, illuminating one side of Bob Garston's face. Charles saw bewilderment, then understanding, quickly followed by fury. "How the hell did you hear about that?"

Charles protected his source. "Let's just say I heard."

"Did my wife tell you?"

"No. I've never met your wife."

"Look, if this gets out to the gossip columns I'll bloody murder you." Realization of what he had said came into Bob Garston's face. It was followed by a twisted smile. "Unfortunate remark perhaps, in the circumstances. So . . . you think I killed Barrett. May I ask how I'm supposed to have done it?"

"Anyone who was round the studio area between six-thirty and six-fifty could have done it. They only needed to take the cyanide from Studio B into Studio A and put it in the glass. Would have taken two minutes, maximum."

Bob Garston nodded grimly.

"You were seen at about twenty-five to seven—coming out of Studio A."

"Yes." He lost his temper. "Dammit! Why the hell did I go in there?"

"You tell me," said Charles.

Bob Garston let out a long sigh. "I didn't do it, you know. I didn't kill Barrett."

"No?"

"No, I bloody didn't!"

"Then why are you getting so upset?"

"Because, as I said, I'm the obvious suspect. The same day you tell the police Chippy didn't do it, they're going to be round knocking on my door, asking questions. It'll be down the station, 'helping with enquiries' . . . they might even bloody arrest me."

"But if you can prove you're innocent—"

"Doesn't make a blind bit of difference. Look, my career's at an important stage, could take off quite dramatically in the next couple of months. The last thing I need now is my name over the papers."

"But, as I said, if you can prove you're innocent—"

"Listen. If there's one thing doing my sort of programme has taught me, it's that mud sticks. I make some allegation on the show, however oblique it is, about some official, and that bloke never lives it down. He's lost credibility . . . his colleagues don't trust him any more. I know, I've got plenty of letters to prove it. I've even been sued a few times. Once the allegation's been made, no amount of public denial can make it go away completely. Look at the newspapers— thousands read the scandalous headline—how many read the little printed apology for getting the facts wrong that comes out the next week?"

Under other circumstances, Charles might have questioned the assurance with which Joe Soap admitted destroying the credibility of his victims, but it wasn't the moment for moral debate. "Well, I'm glad you're aware of the stakes," he said. "So now perhaps you realize that the only way for you to keep the police off your doorstep is to prove to our satisfaction that you are innocent."

"Oh, I am."

"Good. Tell us why, and then perhaps you can help us find out who did kill Barrett Doran."

"Right." Bob Garston was clearly ill at ease as the subject of interrogation, and made a bid to take over the interview himself. In his best hectoring manner, he demanded, "You want to know what I was doing between six-thirty and six-thirty-five that evening?"

"Yes. We know you went into Studio A."

"All right, all right. I did. I'm not denying it."

"Why?"

"Don't rush me. I'm about to bloody tell you, aren't I?" He paused, as if composing his next sentence into the most palatable form. "The fact is, I wanted to get on to that set. I wanted to stand by Barrett's lectern. I just wanted to get the feel of it . . . to know what it felt like to be in charge of that kind of show. You know, just like a little lad trying on his Dad's overalls. . . ."

This winsome simile would have gone down well with the *Joe Soap* audience, but it failed to charm Charles. "That doesn't sound very convincing to me. And I'm not sure that the police would be that convinced either."

"Well, it happens to be the bloody truth!" Bob Garston snapped petulantly. "I can't help it if the truth isn't convincing, can I?"

"I'm only thinking of you, Bob," said Charles with needling magnanimity. "You're the one who wants to keep the police off your doorstep. Of course, they may be convinced by this story of whimsical role-playing, but I doubt—"

"Look!" Bob Garston pointed an angry finger in his antagonist's face. "You just asked me why I went in. I told you. What happened when I got there is a different question.

There was no way that I could have fiddled around with Barrett's glass. I'd have been seen."

"There was someone else in there?"

"Of course there bloody was!"

"Who? The contestant, Tim Dyer? Hadn't he left?"

"No. Not him. It was the designer, wasn't it? Him with the bloody stupid haircut. He was there, fiddling with his precious set."

"Sylvian," murmured Sydnee, breaking her long silence.

"So what did you do?" asked Charles.

"Well, I wasn't going to start prancing round, pretending to be the host, was I? Not with him there. I turned straight round and walked out again."

Charles's mind was racing as he voiced a formal thanks.

"Don't think I told you because I wanted to. But just bloody see that when you do go to the police, you tell them I'm out of the bloody reckoning. I haven't worked this hard on my career to have it shot to pieces by some half-baked rumour." Without waiting for any response, he turned round to Sydnee. "Right, with that out of the way, perhaps we'd better go and talk about this bloody game show." He leant across Charles and clicked open the passenger door. "You can get out and walk."

Charles got out. And, as he walked the three miles back to Hereford Road, he thought again and again of what Barrett Doran had said about Sylvian de Beaune's first television set design.

Chapter Eleven

SYLVIAN DE BEAUNE'S flat was at the top of an old converted warehouse in what used to be London's Dockland. It was up four flights of stairs and there was no Entryphone, so a long gap ensued between their ring on the bell and his appearance at the front door.

He looked surprised to see them, recognizing Sydnee, but apparently never having seen Charles before in his life. He had put in further work on his appearance. The black Mohican strip on his head now had orange tufts at the front, and clusters of orange feathers depended from his ears. His face was covered with white make-up, relieved only by a dab of orange on the lips and eyelids. He was out of the leather gear now, and dressed in a kind of pyjamas of off-white sackcloth, joined at the seams by beige leather thongs. The effect was, to Charles, reminiscent of a line-drawing of medieval underwear from one of his school text-books with a title like *Social Life in the Middle Ages*. He was coming to the conclusion that, amongst other things, Sylvian de Beaune designed his own clothes.

It was clear, when they got upstairs, that he was his own interior designer as well. The flat was really one long room, whose exposed rafters under a pitched roof should have given it the appearance of a Saxon mead-hall. And would have given it the appearance of a Saxon mead-hall if every surface had not been painted silver. The floor had been painted the same colour, and what must have been lovely views over the Thames were excluded by silver paint over the panes of the high windows. The area was lit by theatrical spotlights, the harshness of whose glare was subdued by gels of red and blue. Their beams were trained on to matt-black rectangular boxes, which, by a process of elimination, Charles deduced to be furniture (though which was a table and which a chair he would not like to have had to specify).

Sydnee showed no surprise at the surroundings, which must mean either that she had been there before, or that all her colleagues lived in similar environments. (If the second were the case, it was not surprising that the three researchers had found the Hereford Road bedsitter a little unusual.)

On one of the matt-black shapes a sheet of paper was pinned, and the selection of pens, templates and rulers nearby suggested that Sylvian had been working on his latest design when interrupted by the doorbell. Charles did not dare to contemplate what it might be.

As they entered, music, which could either have been South American flutes or a team of asthmatics competitively blowing blockages out of hose-pipes, sounded loudly. Sylvian de Beaune went across to a matt-black box with an array of matt-black buttons on the front, and moderated the volume.

He gestured to them to sit. Charles had almost fully descended when he heard the words, "No. That's a table", and moved accordingly to a smaller matt-black box.

Sylvian remained standing. "What is it, Sydnee?"

"If The Cap Fits."

"Don't tell me—John Mantle wants more bloody changes?"

"No. It's harking back to the first pilot."

"Oh yes?"

"Barrett Doran's death."

Had there been any natural colour in Sylvian de Beaune's face, that would have bleached it out. He gaped, stupefied.

"Chippy didn't kill him," Sydnee continued. Because he

140

still seemed incapable of speech, she persisted, "Charles here drank from Barrett's glass at about six-thirty. At that point it definitely contained gin."

"Oh, my God." The words were hardly audible.

Charles picked up the initiative. "So the cyanide was put in the glass after that time. You were seen in the studio just after six-thirty by Bob Garston."

The orange lips moved, but this time no sound came out.

"It was your first major set, isn't that right, Sylvian? You were very proud of it, very worried about it. We know what Barrett Doran said when he saw it for the first time. Not very appreciative of your efforts, was he?"

Still no words came, but the designer shook his head, as if in disbelief. Slowly, he subsided on to one of the matt-black rectangular boxes. It was the one he had said was a table, but Charles didn't think it was the moment to say anything. He and Sydnee maintained the silence.

Finally, Sylvian de Beaune spoke. His voice was dull, as if he were repeating something learned by rote. "I hoped it hadn't happened. I went into a terrible state of panic when he died and I heard it was cyanide. But then when Chippy was arrested, and I heard about how she had a motive to kill him and the opportunity to get the poison, I thought it was all right. I thought he'd got the right glass."

"The right glass? Did you put the cyanide in it?"

The black and orange tufted head shook. "No. Why on earth should I do that? No, that's not what I did."

"Then what did you do?"

The voice retained its monotone as he told them. "As you say, it was my first major set. As you say, I was worried about it. I kept looking at it from different angles, kept trying to see things that didn't work. That's why I went back into the studio during the meal-break. I was worried that something had looked wrong, so I went in to check."

"What were you worried about—the wheel?" asked

Charles, remembering what Tim Dyer had done to that part of the set.

"No. There was just something in the colours that had looked wrong. Something wrong with the balance between the lectern and the celebrities' desk. I'd looked and looked at it, and eventually the only thing I could think of was the glasses—the four on the desk and the one on the lectern."

"But they were all the same—surely?"

"They were all *nearly* the same, yes. But they had been specially made to match the set. Hand-painted. I thought maybe they were slightly different, maybe there was more red on one, more blue on another. It was only likely to be a tiny difference, but something definitely looked wrong and I couldn't think of anything else."

"So what did you do?" asked Charles, with a sick feeling that he knew what the answer was going to be.

His worst fears were confirmed. "I started changing them round."

"Oh, my God."

"Just to see if it made the colour balance better."

"So which one did you change with Barrett's?" asked Charles, resigned.

"I can't remember."

"Oh, come on. You must remember," Charles snapped. "You realize how important this is, don't you?"

"Yes. I do. Now. But, honestly, I can't remember. I tried them every way. I moved first one and then the other. I really couldn't say at the end which one was where. That's why I felt so awful when I heard about the cyanide. And then, when Chippy was arrested, I thought, thank God, at least he got the right one back."

"Except that his right one contained gin at six-thirty."

"Yes." The tufted head drooped.

"But surely," said Sydnee excitedly, "the police would have checked the glasses afterwards. If we go to them and say what happened, and find out who had the one containing gin—"

Charles shook his head. "The desk got knocked over. The glasses were scattered all over the place."

Sylvian raised his head. "Yes, I don't understand that. I designed it to be very stable. I mean, the centre of gravity was—"

But Sydnee didn't think it was the moment for a discussion of the intricacies of furniture design. "Surely, Charles, the celeb who had gin in his or her glass would have noticed?"

"Must've done, yes. But nobody's said anything, have they? Otherwise Chippy wouldn't have been arrested. Which must mean the intended victim knew the poison was meant for him—"

"Or for her."

"Yes . . . and is deliberately keeping quiet about it."

"And all the while letting Chippy suffer," said Sydnee, boiling with resentment.

"You realize something else . . . ?"

Sydnee looked at him curiously.

"If the cyanide wasn't put into Barrett's glass but into someone else's, it could have been done at any time during the meal-break."

"Oh no. And all our checking of people's movements has been quite worthless."

Charles nodded, then let out a long sigh. "I think we're going to have to get our little research team together again, Sydnee."

Chapter Twelve

NO ONE EVEN suggested that the second meeting of Charles's research team should take place in his bedsitter. They met instead at Harry Cockers, where Sydnee, Chita and Quentin obviously felt much more at ease.

"Isn't it a bit of a risk," Charles had said when the idea was mentioned, "talking about this sort of thing in such a public place?"

"Good God, no," Sydnee had replied airily. "It's ideal. Perfect security. Nobody at Harry Cockers goes to listen to anyone else. They just go to listen to themselves."

And, as he once again sat watching the screeching variegated flying-suits at the bar, Charles had to admit she was right.

He had asked Sydnee to view the tape of the ill-fated pilot, concentrating on two specific moments, and the first business of their meeting was her report on this.

"I'm afraid it didn't help, Charles. The trouble is, television's such a selective medium. You only see the shots that the director chooses and that the vision-mixer punches up. What you were hoping to see probably happened off-camera."

"There must have been shots of the celebrities drinking."

"Oh yes. There are. But in none of them are they showing any unusual reaction."

"But come on, if you pick up a glass you think contains water and take a swig from it and find it contains gin, you *must* react. There's no way you can help yourself."

144

"You're probably right. And I expect someone did react like that, but the fact remains that the camera wasn't on them while they did it."

"Damn." Another hope bubbled up in his mind. "Did any of them not drink at all? That might be as much of a pointer as a reaction to the first swig. Once they'd identified the gin—"

The copper-beech hair swished as Sydnee shook her head apologetically. "No. All four of them take a drink from their glass at least once while they're in shot."

"One of them must have been covering up," Quentin drawled.

"Covering up what?" asked Charles.

"As soon as the person in question smelt the gin, he or she must have realized what had happened, realized that the cyanide glass had been switched and that someone else was going to cop it. So they'd want to hide the fact that they knew anything about it."

Charles grimaced. "Sorry, Quentin, that doesn't work. The only person who knew there was a glass with cyanide in it was the person who put it there. Unless we're talking about an elaborate suicide plot, the discovery by that person that he or she had gin would not automatically mean that the proposed murder victim's glass had been switched. They'd just think, funny, why have I got gin in here?"

"But why wouldn't they have mentioned it when questioned by the police? Surely then the police would have realized there was something odd and—"

"No. You see, by then the proposed murder victim would know what had happened. As soon as Barrett Doran reacted to the poison, they must have understood, and realized why they had gin in their glass. But, for some reason of their own, they didn't want the police to know that someone was out to kill them. Which was why they upset the table—to send all the glasses over the floor and confuse the evidence."

He looked across at Sydnee, who shook her head lugubriously. "Camera wasn't on it. There's a shot of the celebs before Barrett takes his fatal swig, then the camera stays with him as he starts choking. Next time we see the celebs, they're running forward and the desk's already tipped over."

"So we've no idea who pushed it?"

"No."

"Because that person, I'll lay any money, was the intended victim." Charles looked at Chita and Quentin. "You two were on the set. You didn't by any chance see . . . ?"

His words trickled to a stop as they shook their heads. "Sorry. There was so much confusion and chaos that we didn't really see anything."

Sydnee spoke. "Joanie Bruton said it was Nick Jeffries who pushed the desk over."

"Yes."

"Any reason to disbelieve her?"

Charles shrugged. "Not really, but I'm now getting so paranoid about this case that I'm suspicious of everyone."

"On the new time-scale, of course," Quentin announced slowly, "Nick Jeffries would have had time to put the cyanide in a glass himself."

"Yes, but I think the person who pushed the desk over was the intended victim rather than the murderer."

Sydnee corrected him. "Not necessarily, Charles. As soon as Barrett Doran had started choking, the murderer would have realized that something had gone wrong and have exactly the same reason to confuse the evidence as the intended victim."

Charles was forced to admit the truth of this.

"In fact, a much more straightforward reason than the intended victim."

He was forced to admit the truth of that too. He looked round at his researchers. "Right, so Nick Jeffries is now in

146

the running. Who else? Back we go to the tedious business of retracing everyone's footsteps."

"We've done it," said Chita, and handed him a blue folder.

Charles looked at her in surprise.

"Well, we knew you'd want to know, so we got together and went through everyone. We are professional researchers, you know."

"Yes. Of course." He opened the folder and looked at the list inside. It read as follows:

SUSPECTS WITH OPPORTUNITY

1. BOB GARSTON—Left Conference Room at 6.05. Not seen again until 6.20 when he was observed by Tim Dyer walking along the corridor with Roger Bruton.

2. JOANIE BRUTON—Left Conference Room at 6.10 with Roger to go to Make-up, where he left her. According to Make-up, left them at 6.20. Roger Bruton claims she met him by the lifts a little before 6.30. By that time both of them were back up in the celebrity Conference Room.

3. ROGER BRUTON—See above. On his own after depositing his wife in Make-up. Seen with Bob Garston by Tim Dyer at 6.20. Again presumably on his own until meeting his wife again just before 6.30.

4. NICK JEFFRIES—Left celebrity Conference Room, following Fiona Wakeford, just after 6.15. Seen entering her dressing room at about 6.20, and seen leaving it again about a minute later. Not back in the Conference Room until just after 6.30.

NOTE: These are the facts as accurately as they can be ascertained. They do not, however, take into account the possibility of any of the witnesses lying, nor of a conspiracy amongst any of the above to poison the water glass.

"But just a minute," said Charles, as he finished reading the document. "Surely there are a couple more we should be considering. The two contestants, Tim Dyer and Trish Osborne. They both left their Conference Room at six-fifteen. She went to Barrett Doran's dressing room, but was out of there by twenty-five past and . . ."

Chita shook her head. "She's in the clear. She went straight to the Ladies. One of the Assistant Stage Managers was in there and saw her, trying to repair her make-up. She'd been crying, apparently. She was there till after half-past."

Charles felt obscurely relieved that Trish had been telling the truth. "But what about Tim Dyer?"

Quentin shook his head. "No. We've found another witness there too. One of the dressers saw him hanging around the corridor, looking suspicious. There've been quite a lot of costumes going missing recently, so the dresser watched what he was up to. Tim Dyer went into Studio A just before half-past, but he quite definitely did not go into Studio B."

"So he couldn't have got the cyanide. Oh well, at least thank God that's two of them eliminated." Charles looked down at their list. "Thanks for this. Good bit of work." He sighed ruefully. "I don't know. Bloody marvellous, isn't it? Four murder suspects and I don't even know who they were trying to kill."

"I'm sorry," he said to Sydnee later that evening. "I'm not proving to be much use to you. I'm afraid my reputation as a detective has been a little over-inflated."

She did not deny this, but told him that at least she had been glad of someone to talk to about the case. They were

148

sitting over coffee after dinner in a Covent Garden Italian restaurant. Charles felt very low. The first snagging self-doubts of depression threatened. When the depression came, it could be a long one.

He sighed. "So I suppose now we do what we should have done in the first place—go to the police about it. I tell them that Barrett Doran's glass contained gin at six-thirty. At least that'll let Chippy off the hook."

"And then the police will get on to Sylvian," Sydnee said listlessly. "And he won't be able to tell them which glass he changed for which, because he fiddled about with all of them. . . ."

"But at least sorting out all these bloody suspects then becomes the police's problem. It is their job, after all. That's what they're trained for."

Sydnee nodded and was silent for a moment. "Of course, the police aren't going to be terribly pleased with you."

"What do you mean?"

"Withholding evidence. Why didn't you go and tell them what you knew earlier?"

Charles shrugged. "That's a risk I'll have to take." But he didn't warm to the idea.

"I just feel we've got so close to it," said Sydnee doggedly.

"Oh yes. I thought we were getting close with Bob, but after finding out about the glasses being switched, I don't know, the whole case is so wide open that everything we've done seems to have been wasted."

"Not everything."

"What do you mean?"

"We now know our suspects pretty well. We know what makes them tick, what their priorities are."

"Yes." In spite of himself, Charles felt a flicker of interest. "So where does that lead us?"

"Well, it enables us to think of reasons why they might want to murder each other."

"Go on."

"All right, let's start with Bob Garston. We worked out a lot of reasons why he might want to murder Barrett. In doing that, we should have found out enough about his character to see reasons why he might want to murder someone else."

"His character seems very simple to me. Totally selfish. He's motivated solely by considerations of his career. Anyone who threatened that might be expendable. But Barrett was the only one on the show who represented any kind of threat."

"Maybe. Bob was also desperately worried about adverse publicity."

"That's just another facet of the same thing. It threatened his career." Charles mused in silence for a moment. "The thing that really seemed to get him uptight was that we knew about Barrett and his wife. . . ."

"Yes, he didn't want the gossip columns to get hold of that, did he?"

"No." Charles found his mind wasn't as exhausted as he'd thought. It was waking up again, starting to make connections. "And before the show, the only person he thought knew about the affair was Joanie Bruton . . ."

"And Roger. Remember, Tim overheard Roger talking about it."

"Yes. My God, do you suppose that what Roger was actually saying was a blackmail demand? You do something for us or we'll tell the press about Barrett and your wife."

"It's possible."

"Far-fetched, though. Why should someone as successful as Joanie Bruton want to resort to blackmail?"

"People are greedy. Even the rich—particularly those who've just become rich—always want that little bit more. And Joanie's success may not be that secure. Okay, she's Flavour of the Month at the moment, but we both know how quickly television faces go out of fashion. Then she'd be just back to the journalism. It's not as if she writes books or has got any other nice little earner going for her."

"No." Charles thought about it. "And Joanie is of course ideally placed as a blackmailer. As she said, she's a repository for a great many secrets."

"Exactly."

There was a new excitement in Sydnee's pale-blue eyes. Charles gave her a wry smile. "I can see what you're doing. You're just trying to get me interested in the case again, aren't you?"

"So what's wrong with that?"

"What's wrong with that is that I have so far spent a fortnight getting precisely nowhere, while what I should have done was to go to the police straight away."

"Don't you like a challenge, Charles?"

"I have been challenged and I have shown myself unequal to the challenge."

"Doesn't that frustrate you?"

"Of course it bloody does!" he snapped.

"It certainly frustrates me." This was a new Sydnee, her surface poise giving way to a girlish stubbornness. "I'm a researcher, and the aim of research is to get to the bottom of things, to get to the truth. Nothing pisses me off more than failing in that quest. Go on, you must feel the same. If you don't find out who the murderer is, you're going to be really pissed off, aren't you?"

Charles couldn't deny it.

"Then let's bloody find out who it is. Look, we've already got a motive for Bob to want to kill Joanie. Let's see if we can get any motivations for the rest of them."

Charles was thoroughly hooked again by now.

"Well, the new entrant into the suspect stakes is of course Nick Jeffries. He didn't seem to have a particularly benevolent nature, but I'm not sure I see him as a murderer. Still, let's try and think who he might want to murder."

"Fiona, for refusing his advances?"

"Seems extreme."

"Very sensitive plant, the male ego."

"You don't have to tell me," said Charles ruefully. "On the other hand, I don't really see poison as Nick Jeffries' style. I can see him thumping someone, but . . . Still, I suppose it's possible." He shook his head in frustration. "Oh, I'd just like to see them all together again. I'm sure I'd get some feeling of what they felt for each other if I did."

"You'll have the chance tomorrow."

"What do you mean?"

"It's the second pilot. You may see something."

"Yes, I suppose I may. I must say I'd rather see the first one again. I don't mean the tape. I mean the whole thing. I'm sure if I could see their reactions to the drink or who knocked the desk over, I'd be able to . . ."

He stopped. Sydnee looked at him curiously. She was even more curious when she saw the beatific smile which had spread across his features.

"What on earth is it?"

"Sydnee," he said with a new, calm confidence, "I have had an idea."

Chapter Thirteen

THE DAY OF preparation for the second pilot of *If The Cap Fits* closely followed the pattern of the first, though generally everything was more efficient. John Mantle had gathered an experienced game-show team around him and they had learned from the shortcomings of the previous pilot.

As a result, three Conference Rooms had been booked, so that the "professions" did not have to spend the afternoon pondering Sydnee's "Ugly Wall". (On this occasion the researchers had assembled a shepherd, a metallurgist, a coach-driver and a vicar, the last of whom thought, mistakenly, that his appearance on the programme would help to make the Church seem more accessible to ordinary people.) The hide-and-seek game of keeping the various participant groups apart was better orchestrated, so that there were less sudden rushes for cover.

An acrimonious confrontation between John Mantle and the Head of Wardrobe had resulted in the hats being ready when required (though the sullen expressions on the faces of the staff who produced them suggested that they still did not think it was their job). However, arguments could not be avoided on the subject of what sort of hats metallurgists wore and whether a Church of England vicar could really be properly identified by a biretta.

Sydnee had had a long session with Make-up and finally organized a schedule that would get everyone done without transgressing the sacred and expensive lines of the meal-break.

The new contestants spent the afternoon in the same state of nervous tension as their predecessors. The extrovert personalities for which they had been selected seemed to desert them once on the set, leading Aaron Greenberg and Dirk van Henke, who had just returned from a long lunch at Inigo Jones with John Mantle, to turn on him and object that this bunch had even less "pazazz" than the last lot.

They were also suspicious of Bob Garston's "pazazz"-rating. His gritty Northern approach to the job of host contrasted unfavourably with the more flamboyant style of "Eddie back in the States", and John Mantle had to endure a further barrage of talk about killing Golden Geese stone-dead and screwing up something which could mean "someone making a pot". As ever, he trimmed and shifted, full of magnanimous concessions which gave away nothing. He could see the end in sight. The next day, come what might, the Americans would be on Concorde on their way back home. The massive accumulations of their bill at the Savoy and the charges on his Gold Card would be at an end, and John Mantle would at last have some time to himself.

He felt confident that, by the time that magic moment arrived, he would also have the makings of a very successful game-show series which would run for years. As Sydnee had suggested, for him, having to do a second pilot had been like a gift from heaven. It had given him the opportunity to adjust the format, to regulate the pace of the show and give the whole package an additional gloss. Good housekeeper to the end, he was even confident that his budget would not suffer too much. Whereas there had been almost no possibility (even without Barrett Doran's murder) of the first pilot being transmitted, there was a good chance that the second could be, probably not as the first of the series, but safely tucked away four or five into the run. All in all, John Mantle was very pleased with the way things had turned out. Barrett Doran's death couldn't have come at a better time for him.

It was a subject that was not mentioned in the celebrity Conference Room. The foursome reverted to the required laid-back approach to the proceedings. The three who had played the game before had good reason to take it lightly; they now knew the format so well there was no need even to pretend to be doing any homework on it. Joanie and Roger Bruton muttered their way through a file of correspondence. Fiona Wakeford painted her fingernails with studious concentration. Nick Jeffries, whom this studious concentration was intended to exclude, sat around restlessly looking at a newspaper and resorting too often to the hip-flask in his pocket.

The newcomer, brought in to fill the gap on the panel left by Bob Garston's promotion, was George Birkitt. He was an actor with whom Charles Paris had worked on numerous occasions. Of moderate talent, he had been elevated by appearances in various television series to celebrity status. Since he was devoid of personality, he had no inner star quality, but was content to assume the mannerisms and behaviour of authentic stars he had met. The act was successful, in that the television audience seemed unable to distinguish him from the genuine article.

George Birkitt joined in the occasional, insouciant banter of the Conference Room, saying things like, "Never sure about these damned game shows myself. Still, the agent says they're good, keep the old face in front of the public, show there's a man behind the actor. So I suppose I should take his advice. After all, that's what I pay the old sod such a large chunk of my income for . . ."

He did, however, refer to his copy of the show's format rather more often than was strictly proper for someone of his celebrity status.

Between the Conference Rooms Jeremy Fowler flitted, a lost soul trying to shed his burden of wacky one-liners about shepherds, metallurgists, coach-drivers, vicars and hats. He found few takers, though George Birkitt, who recognized that he had the imaginative faculty of a bar of soap, did scribble down an old joke about a rockstar's school cap being discovered when he had a haircut.

And all the while Bob Garston dashed about the place, expending enormous energy and charm. He was determined to show not only that he could host the show a damned sight better than Barrett Doran, but also that he could be lovable with it. The effort he put into his affability was almost physically painful.

In Studio A rehearsal wound on its dilatory way. Jim Trace-Smith exhorted the participants to bravura performances with all the damp aplomb of fruit juice soaking through a paper bag.

And Sylvian de Beaune, dressed for the occasion in a leopard-skin T-shirt and gold lamé trousers, fussed around his set and wondered why Sydnee had asked him to meet Charles Paris for a chat in the bar at half-past six.

For Charles it was a day of nerves. Not terrified, panicky nerves, but nerves of anticipation, that jumpy surging twitchiness which precedes a first night, the feeling that a great many different strands are coming together and that if one can only keep going a little longer, everything will be all right.

This state covered the whole spectrum of emotion and included moments of great confidence. In one of these, he rang Maurice Skellern, assertively demanding what there was coming up on the work front.

The fact that his agent gave the predictable reply, "Nothing. Very quiet at the moment, Charles", did not instantly deflate his mood, so he made another audacious phone-call. He rang the number of Frances's school and asked to speak to the headmistress.

"What on earth is it?" Her voice was tight with anxiety. "Something to do with Juliet or the boys?"

It was predictable that her first thought should be for their daughter and grandchildren, though why she should think he might know anything of Juliet's troubles Charles could not imagine. If there were anything wrong, Juliet would have got straight on to Frances. Experience had not encouraged her to rely on her father.

"No, Frances. It's just me ringing to say hello."

"You know I'm at work."

"I told you never to ring me at the office," hissed Charles in the voice he'd used as a panicked adulterer in a tired bedroom farce at Blackpool ("If it's laughter you're after, stay at home and watch television."—*Liverpool Daily Post*).

"I've got someone with me," she said in the frosty voice of reprimand which was much imitated by her fourth-formers.

"I want to see you."

"We met a couple of weeks ago."

"I know. It's habit-forming. I want to see you again. Another dinner?"

"Well . . ."

"Name a date. Any evening you like. Except tonight."

"Next Wednesday. The Italian place."

"I'll book."

"You certainly will. Eight-thirty. On the dot. Or forget it."

The headmistress put the phone down on him, but that didn't extinguish the little spark of excitement inside. If he and Frances really could get together again . . . He was in his fifties, too old for self-dramatizing actresses, too old for desperate housewives in Billericay. Maybe this time it really would work again with Frances . . . Why not, after all? They were both mature human beings, both knew the score. The separation had enriched their relationship in some ways. If he was patient, if he was sensible, he was sure it could work. . . .

He went from the payphone on the landing into his bedsitter. He made a pretence at reading and resisted the temptation to have a drink. No, need all his wits about him later.

There was nothing he could do until the evening. He just hoped that Sydnee had done her stuff.

Chapter Fourteen

SYDNEE HAD DONE the first bit of her stuff, anyway. When Charles arrived at the Reception of W.E.T. House and identified himself, the girl, the same one as on his previous visit, immediately handed him an envelope which contained a ticket to that night's recording of a brand-new big-prize game show, *If The Cap Fits*, together with a Visitor's Security Pass, stamped for that day only.

This latter document meant that, rather than joining the queue of Townswomen's Guild, insurance company social club and amateur dramatic society members round the back of the building, he could go inside to the bar.

It was a little before six-thirty. He bought himself a large Bell's and stood alone sipping it, a sore thumb amidst the tight fists of programme groups. Flying-suits giggled and gesticulated, disparaging rival productions, reliving location disasters, calculating overtime payments, repeating the day's insults.

Sylvian arrived promptly. He was not wearing make-up for the day in the studio, so the shiny pallor of his face was his own. His eyes flickered about the bar. He refused the offer of a drink.

Charles reminded the designer of something he had said in his silver Dockland flat. Sylvian, expecting a completely different line of questioning, readily answered Charles's query about the celebrities' blue desk on the set of *If The Cap Fits*.

Their conversation lasted less than two minutes. The ice in Charles's glass had not had time to melt before he drained the whisky and went down to Studio A.

It was about quarter to seven. The studio was empty and still. No one yet had come back from their meal-break. The red, blue and silver set gleamed under working lights. The cameras were pointed at cards on caption-stands, ready for the half-hour's line-up time, due to start at seven. Air-conditioning hummed slightly, and gave the atmosphere a surprising chill, before the full lighting and crowds of people would warm it up.

Charles walked on to the familiar set, but he did not go to the side where he had stood two weeks before with the hamburger chef, the surgeon and the stockbroker. He walked round the back of the long blue desk where the celebrities would sit, and looked under it. It was exactly as Sylvian had said.

Next he inspected the four blue-and-red-striped glasses, which stood on the desk in front of each red chair.

He also looked at the other glass and the carafe on the host's lectern.

All were empty.

Good. Sydnee was continuing to do her stuff.

She had advised him to watch from the area just to the right of the block of audience seating. This was where the Stage Managers, who shared their power on studio days with the Floor Managers, and the Make-up girls, who were poised to leap on with saving puffs of powder, stood during recordings. The advantage of the position was that it commanded an uninterrupted view of the centre of the set. From any of the audience seats the outlook would be interrupted by cameras and their operators, sound men and Floor Managers.

The members of the audience entered at various speeds. A party later to be identified as the St Richard's Church Youth Club scuttered in on a cloud of giggles. A works rugby club, who had met for a few jars in the pub beforehand, thumped noisily down the stairs to their seats. A Senior Citizens' Day

Group wheezed in arthritically with much clattering of sticks. Once seated, they all decided they needed to go to the lavatory before the recording started, and wheezed out again. Some of the rugby club members also went off to lose a few pints.

Charles was only partly aware of these commotions. He kept his eyes firmly on the set. At one point Sydnee flashed round the corner of it. She gave him a quick grin and a thumbs-up before going back to calm the nerves of her shepherd, metallurgist, coach-driver and vicar.

Sharp at half-past seven, when most of the audience were back from the lavatories (though some of the Senior Citizens' Day Group were still waiting in the queue that had built up in the Ladies), Charlie Hook bounced on stage, picked up a microphone and started to tell them all how lovely they were.

It was a lovely show they were going to see, too, he assured them. Indeed, everything was lovely. He welcomed a few lovely parties, exchanged a few lovely innuendoes with the rugby club and indulged in a little lovely banter with one lovely Senior Citizen making her way back from the Ladies.

Then, on a "speed-it-up" signal from the Floor Manager, he moved on to the introductions. "And our host for tonight's show is a really lovely feller—somebody you all know and love from your television screen as Mr Joe Soap— well, here he is tonight without the Joe—and without the soap either . . . ladies and gentlemen, give a lovely warm round of applause to . . . Mr—Bob—Garston!"

A lovely warm round of applause was duly given, as the show's new host strode on, oozing common touch from every pore. He grinned ruggedly at the audience and exchanged a few gritty pleasantries with them.

He gave a brief outline of what the game was about, but said it was basically very simple and they'd have no problem picking it up as they went along. Then he distributed accolades to the "boffins in the back-room", without whom the show would not be possible. He praised the humour of Jim Trace-Smith and the organizing skill of John Mantle, before moving on to introduce "tonight's celebrity panel".

Charles tensed as they came on and sat in their appointed seats. Nick Jeffries shadow-boxed at the audience, much to their delight. Fiona Wakeford simpered at them, which they found equally rewarding. Joanie Bruton marched on, looking sensible, bright, but nonetheless feminine (and many of the female Senior Citizens turned to each other to comment on how sensible, bright, but nonetheless feminine she was). George Birkitt came on grinning and gave a wave, secure in the familiarity of his television face.

Bob Garston then introduced "the plucky foursome who, believe it or not, have actually volunteered to take part in this circus", and the contestants, propelled by the unseen hand of Chita, came blinking on to the set.

In the Gallery, Aaron Greenberg looked at Dirk van Henke, then, accusingly, at John Mantle. "About as much 'pazazz' as a wet noodle," he grumbled.

John Mantle smiled evenly.

It was nearly seven forty-five. The lovely Nikki and the lovely Linzi, after final checks at the straps of their bikinis, took up their positions by the prizes. The Senior Floor Manager stepped forward to tell Bob Garston to wind it up and get ready to record. Charlie Hook instructed the audience to wait for an applause cue from him and to watch the opening credits on the monitors above their heads.

The clock for the beginning of Part One appeared in shot. The one-minute countdown began.

Twenty-five seconds in, Nick Jeffries started waving in distress.

He had gone to have a drink from his red-and-blue-striped glass and discovered it to be empty.

The Senior Floor Manager looked annoyed at the delay. Charlie Hook came forward to reassure the audience that they were still lovely. A hustled-looking Floor Manager came on to the set with a jug on a tray. He poured liquid into the four celebrities' glasses, then crossed to the lectern and filled Bob Garston's. The remains of his jugful went into the carafe.

He scurried off and the Senior Floor Manager bustled forward for the restart of the recording. They must get moving, he insisted, they were wasting time. No more breaks, please. Must get on with it.

He got the message that the video-recording was stable, and the clock once again appeared on the monitors. This time it ran the full minute, disappearing just before the animated credits and music began.

Charles Paris stared across at the celebrities' desk. The concentration made his eyes hurt.

Nick Jeffries, who had been the one who wanted a drink, took a swig from his glass. Charles noted his expression with satisfaction.

Good old Sydnee. She'd done her stuff, all right.

The prizes for the second pilot were a gas-fired barbecue, over which the lovely Nikki draped herself lasciviously, a week's holiday for two in Eilat, and the Austin Metro (which Tim Dyer reckoned should by rights be his), from which the lovely Linzi once again waved. The audience oohed and aahed and applauded appropriately.

While the credits were running, Joanie Bruton took a sip from her red-and-blue-striped glass. Charles Paris noted her reaction.

Bob Garston introduced the celebrities with suitable jocularity. George Birkitt tried to launch into his joke about a rock-star having a haircut, but was cut short by the smiling host. Disgruntled, the actor took a drink from his glass. Though it was not relevant to his enquiry, Charles Paris noted George Birkitt's expression.

The shepherd, the metallurgist, the coach-driver and the vicar all came on wearing inappropriate hats. With celebrity help (and, in Aaron Greenberg's view, with total lack of "pazazz"), the contestants changed the hats round. Three of them identified the metallurgist as a vicar. It was all very riotous. At the end of Round One, one contestant was eliminated, but she didn't go away empty-handed—no, she took with her a lovely *If The Cap Fits* cap!

The lovely Nikki and the lovely Linzi brought on the hat-boxes for Round Two. The three survivors made their guesses, and another member of the public was put out of contention. But of course he had won himself some money—not to mention his *If The Cap Fits* cap!

It was the End of Part One. None of the celebrities left the set while Charlie Hook re-emphasized the loveliness of the audience and explained that the director would have to take some cutaway shots of the eliminated contestants.

Two celebrities had still to touch their red-and-blue striped glasses.

In Round Three the remaining contestants picked out of the box respectively a Roman helmet and a baseball cap. This meant that they had to answer questions on History and Sport. The first, clearly a man of no judgement but with an eye for a pretty girl, chose Fiona Wakeford to help him on History. The second, slightly shrewder, selected Nick Jeffries as his adviser on Sport.

When her protégé had been eliminated and while he was being told about his *If The Cap Fits* cap, Fiona Wakeford returned to her seat. She sat down and took a drink from her glass. Charles Paris noted her reaction.

There was now only one contestant left and it was time for the *Hats In The Ring* finale, with a chance to win the Super-Duper prize—a brand-new Austin Metro, complete with tax, insurance and a year's supply of petrol!

"Ooh!" sighed the audience, barely able to contain themselves (in fact, completely unable to contain themselves in the case of two of the Senior Citizens, who once again set off noisily for the Ladies).

The surviving contestant stood in the middle of Sylvian de Beaune's red wheel, while Bob Garston explained to her what was to happen.

He gave the wheel an enormous pull to set it spinning, and withdrew to his lectern. Once there, while the audience vociferously willed the wheel to stop with the crown overhead, he copied Barrett Doran's timing and used his red-and-blue-striped glass as a prop to increase the tension of the moment.

He took a long swallow. Charles Paris noted the expression on his face.

The audience sighed in communal disappointment. Above the final contestant's head had come to rest a fez. It was worth another £200 to add to what she had already won—not forgetting, of course, her *If The Cap Fits* cap!

John Mantle was no fool. After the close call of the first pilot, he had summoned Sylvian de Beaune into his office and ordered the designer to fix the wheel so that any hat but the crown ended up on top.

Charles Paris was unaware of that trickery. Nor, at that moment, would he have been interested to hear about it. His mind was too full.

He knew who the intended victim had been on the previous pilot.

And he knew who the murderer was.

He went out into the corridor that led from the dressing rooms. By the lifts was a small Reception area, with a few uncomfortably low armchairs.

In one of them Roger Bruton was sitting.

He looked up at Charles with no particular pleasure.

"Oh. Hello. I'm just waiting for Joanie."

Charles sat down beside him.

"I think I'll wait for her too," he said.

Chapter Fifteen

"I KNOW WHAT happened," said Charles after a long pause.

"Sorry?" Roger Bruton seemed miles away. Charles looked at the weak face, whose baby-like roundness was belied, on close inspection, by an elaborate map of tiny lines. Roger was older than one might at first think. Well over fifty, anyway. And his exquisitely-preserved wife was probably about the same age.

"I know what happened on the last pilot."

The faded brown eyes turned towards him, but still did not look very interested.

"Oh?"

"When Barrett Doran died."

A minimal flicker of alarm came into the eyes, but the tone was still confident as Roger Bruton said, "I'm sorry. I don't know what you're talking about. What happened?"

"Do you think he was killed by the girl, Chippy?"

"As I said when we last discussed it, that is what the police seem to think."

Charles shook his head. "It doesn't work that way. You know, at the end, after Barrett had fallen down, all the celebrities got up and tipped over their desk . . . ?"

"Yes."

"Hard thing to do, overturn that desk."

"Oh?"

"Yes. I've talked to its designer. It's got a low centre of gravity."

"Nick Jeffries is a strong man."

"Hmm. And Joanie quite definitely said that Nick Jeffries was the one who overturned it. But, you see, it's not strength that matters with that desk. It's simple physics . . . levers . . . a matter of applying force at the right point."

"I'm not with you."

"There's a bar along the back. A good upward pull on that would tip the desk over. And it wouldn't take a lot of strength. But you'd have to be the right height to do it unobtrusively. Anyone tall—anyone, say, Nick Jeffries' height—would have to bend right down to the bar."

Roger Bruton did not react, so Charles spelled it out. "Nick Jeffries couldn't have done it. Even in all that confusion someone would have noticed. The only person who could have done it was Joanie."

Roger Bruton attempted bluster. "So? So Joanie knocked the desk over. So what?"

"So she had a reason to do it. She wanted to break all the glasses, create confusion, do anything that would disguise the fact that hers contained gin."

The tired eyes stared hauntedly at Charles, but there were no words.

"I've confirmed that this evening," Charles continued. "By a simple trick. I arranged that all the water-glasses tonight should contain gin. That's why they were empty when the recording started. I didn't want anyone to draw attention to it earlier. Once the show was under way— particularly under way *late*—I knew that no one would dare stop the recording. They'd all just press on. But I also knew that they'd react. It's a shock when you pick up a glass which you believe to contain water and find it's full of gin. No one, however professional a performer, could disguise that initial split-second of shock. No one, that is, who hadn't been warned . . . no one to whom it hadn't happened before."

Roger Bruton remained as still as a corpse.

"The only person who gave no reaction when she discovered the glass contained gin was your wife."

"So . . ." The man's lips hardly moved as he spoke. "What do you reckon that means?"

"Joanie's very quick-witted, isn't she? Her mind moves fast. Quite fast enough on the first pilot to link the fact that Barrett had been poisoned with the fact that her glass contained gin. She knew he always had gin on the set, so it was a fair assumption that the two glasses had been changed round. She also knew that someone hated her enough to want to murder her. But because that person was someone very close to her, she tried to confuse the evidence, so that the truth would never come out."

A long silence hung between them.

"I'm right. Aren't I, Roger?"

Slowly the tension drained out of him. Muscle by muscle, Roger Bruton's body relaxed, till he lay slumped back on the low armchair.

With something that sounded like a little laugh, eventually he said, "Yes. You're right."

"Why?"

The murderer looked at Charles and slowly, wryly, shook his head. "You wouldn't understand."

"No? But Joanie did. Joanie always understood, didn't she? And that was why you hated her."

The faded eyes looked at Charles with a new respect. "Yes," Roger said softly, "that's why."

He paused, gathering his thoughts, before continuing. "No one who hasn't been through it can know what it's like, how smothering, how emasculating it is, always to be understood. Oh, if the understanding is warm, if it's sympathetic, that's different. But when it's clinical, when it treats you like a specimen, a case-history, that's when the hatred builds up.

"It was never a good marriage. The sex side was never . . . Joanie just wasn't interested. Oh, happy enough to give

forthright, frank advice to others, but in our own bed . . .
nothing. That's why we never had children. I wanted children, but if there's no sex, well. . . ." He shrugged. "At first
I had a few affairs, but Joanie always understood. She was
always so bloody understanding, welcomed me back, forgave
me, patronized me, made me feel like a delinquent teenager.
A couple of years of that, and it takes the fun out of
extramarital sex."

"Why didn't you leave her?"

Roger Bruton grimaced hopelessly. "Because I'm weak.
Because she's a stronger personality than I am. Maybe just
because I'm a glutton for punishment. So I stayed with her,
listening to her pontificating hour after hour, listening to her
advise everyone and anyone about their lives, and feeling the
hollowness within my own just growing and growing."

"When did you first think of murdering her?"

He let out a sharp little laugh. "On our honeymoon, I
suppose. When it became clear that I could forget it as far as a
sex-life was concerned. And it was always there, the idea of
killing her, a pleasing fantasy, something I could retreat to
when she became too intolerable. But I suppose it's got worse
over the last few years. As her career's taken off, as she's
more and more omnipresent, as I can't switch on a radio or
television without hearing it, more and more bloody *understanding*."

"But was there any particular reason why suddenly two
weeks ago . . . ?"

Roger shrugged. "I don't know. A feeling that I couldn't
stand it any longer. I don't think the camel can say which is
going to be the final straw, but he sure as hell recognizes it
when it's put on his back."

"You hadn't had a row?"

"Not a major one. No more than usual. We don't really
have rows. For a long time now I've suppressed all my real
feelings."

"I still don't understand why you should suddenly try to kill her."

"No? Opportunity, I suppose. It was a spur of the moment thing. I'd just taken Joanie into Make-up and she'd said a very lovey-dovey farewell to me. It's moments like that I hate her most, when I see a public display of sexuality from someone I know to be totally without sex. I was angry. I walked through Studio B. There was no one about. I saw the bottle of cyanide. I took it, went through to Studio A, emptied the water from her glass into the carafe on the lectern and filled the glass up with poison. I felt very rational and happy. I just couldn't think why I hadn't done it before."

"But you'd never have got away with it. If she had been killed."

The murderer gave another little shrug. "I don't honestly think I'd have cared that much. I'd have been shot of her, that's all that mattered to me. And I'd have been spared what happened afterwards."

"After Barrett's death?"

"Yes."

"Joanie knew what you'd done?"

"Oh yes. Instantly. She worked it out. And guess what . . . ?"

"She was very understanding about it."

Roger Bruton grinned bitterly as he nodded.

There was another silence.

"So what do I do now?"

"The police have to be told the truth. Chippy's got to be released."

"Yes." Roger looked pensive.

"It might only be manslaughter," said Charles encouragingly. "I don't know the law well enough, but maybe when you try to kill one person and ending up killing someone else . . . I don't know, but. . . ."

The murderer shook his head. "Doesn't matter a lot. I don't see myself enjoying prison, somehow."

"What, losing your freedom, you mean?"

"God, no." This he seemed to find really funny. "You can't talk to me about losing my freedom. I lost that the minute I got married. No, what I couldn't face about prison is the visiting."

"Joanie?"

"Understanding me again. No, thank you." He shuddered. Then, in a new, calm voice, he said, "I'll write to the police and tell them exactly what happened. They'll get the letter tomorrow."

"Roger."

They both looked up towards the sound. Joanie, tiny, beautiful, her fur-coat around her, was hurrying along the passage with arms outstretched. "Roger, darling."

He let her get close before he stood up. Then, after giving her a look of such paralysing contempt that it stopped her dead in her tracks, Roger Bruton walked away from his wife in silence, free of her at last.

Chapter Sixteen

ROGER BRUTON'S SUICIDE was announced on the radio two days later. He had cut his wrists in a hot bath in a hotel room. Neatly on the bedside table he had left a letter addressed to the police.

As a result of this, a day later, Caroline Postgate, known to her friends as Chippy, was released from custody and, although the news got little press coverage, the police closed their file of investigation into the murder of Barrett Doran. Few of the public ever noticed that the case did not come to trial. Barrett Doran's popularity at the time of his death had been enormous, but television reputations are as disposable as used tissues. The shows which had brought him to prominence were of the ephemeral sort which never get repeated, so he was quickly forgotten.

The press coverage of Joanie Bruton was considerably more extensive. The irony of an Agony Aunt's husband committing suicide was not lost on the tabloids, but they were quickly made to change their tune. Joanie mounted her own vigorous press campaign, being interviewed whenever possible, describing her reactions to her husband's death. She particularly stressed the tragedy of depressive illness, whose insidious attacks on the mind can be resistant to any amount of love and understanding. Within a week she was once again the darling of the public, her status enriched by suffering. In descriptions of her, to the words "sensible", "bright" and "forthright", the word "plucky" was quickly added.

Her career continued to blossom. She added depression, bereavement and suicide to the special subjects on which she so readily gave advice to anyone and everyone. She presented the pilot of a new television series on sexual problems, which quickly became a series. Its large viewing public explained away their prurient interest by saying it was "good to get these things out in the open". Everyone agreed that Joanie Bruton was the perfect presenter for such a series, "because she was so understanding".

Charles Paris signed on again at the Lisson Grove Unemployment Office the following Monday. As had become a ritual with him, he rang Maurice Skellern before setting out on this mission, just in case there was any prospect of an acting job coming up. There wasn't. His agent assured him that things were still "very quiet", so Charles kept his appointment. He needed some cash. He was taking his wife out to dinner two days later. Must be careful not to drink it all away before then.

It was about half-past eleven on the Wednesday morning when Sydnee phoned, asking if she could buy him a drink "to say thank you". He said he was busy later in the evening, but it would fit in very well if he dropped by W.E.T. House for a drink about half-past six.

At first he couldn't see her in the bar, but then identified a new yellow flying-suit in the middle of a group in the corner. Tentatively, he went across and tapped her on the shoulder.

"Charles. Great. We're celebrating."

"What's happened?"

"Just heard this afternoon. We've got a series!"

"Of *If The Cap Fits*?"

"Yes."

"That was quick."

"A gap in the schedule. John Mantle got it edited and

shown to the powers-that-be as quickly as possible. We've got the go-ahead for a series of thirteen."

"Well done."

"First studio in four weeks, which means we've got to work like hell."

"Getting all the contestants together?"

"Yes. That and a million other things. Finding fifty-two professions who can be identified by their hats is going to be a bit of a headache, for a start."

"I can see that."

"Let me get you a drink, anyway."

"Oh, are you sure I can't—"

"No. My idea. My thank you. What is it?"

"Whisky'd be great. Bell's."

"Chita and Quentin are here. And Sylvian." She pointed into the crowd.

Sylvian heard his name and turned to give Charles a little nod of uninterested recognition. His Mohican strip was all orange now. Chita and Quentin also saw Charles and gave little waves. But they turned back quickly. They were deeply involved in the series, planning, thinking ahead with relish to all the crises which would inevitably arise.

Jim Trace-Smith was in the centre of the group, and Charles could hear him saying, "What really excites me about this project is that it's so much more intelligent than the average game show. I mean, a lot of them are, quite frankly, mindless shit, but *If The Cap Fits* has got so many elements. There's an educational content . . . and a bit of lateral thinking . . . and that all-important factor of pure luck. And then there's the prize element, which ensures healthy competition. No, some of the other giveaway shows I'd quite honestly be ashamed to have my credit on, but this one I really think is going to break new ground in television. . . ."

The group around him nodded their agreement.

"One large Bell's."

"Bless you, Sydnee."

"Well, thanks for all you've done. Really been great." Somehow her words sounded formal. She was back to the professional researcher thanking a contestant for taking part in the show. The real Sydnee Charles had glimpsed from time to time seemed to have gone back into hiding.

"Has Chippy come back to work yet?"

"Sure. And because this series has got to get put together in such a hurry, she's going to be an Assistant Stage Manager on it. You see, they brought in someone else on *Method in Their Murders* while she was . . . away, and that girl's staying there, so it's all worked out very well."

"Yes."

"Actually, she was in the bar earlier. I'm sure she'd like to thank you personally for what you've done."

The pale-blue eyes flickered round until they saw the familiar blond head. It was bent over a drink close to a darker head. The darker head belonged to Bob Garston, who seemed to be taking a very intense interest in his companion.

"Oh. Yes," said Sydnee. "John got Bob to come in this afternoon as soon as he heard about the series. Quite a few things to talk about . . . with the first studio coming up so soon."

Charles looked across at the couple, and wondered if he was seeing Chippy's unerring instinct for unsuitable men coming into play once again.

"I'm sure you could go and interrupt them, Charles. I mean, as I said, she's dying to say a personal thank you."

"Oh, there's no hurry . . ."

Sydnee didn't press it.

They talked in a desultory fashion, but there didn't seem that much to talk about. Charles recognized what was happening. He'd experienced it before at the end of television series. For three months, or longer, you work intensely closely with a group of people, their concerns become your

175

concerns, you are bound together by the overriding impera-
tive of the programme. You spend all your time with them.
You work with them, eat with them, not uncommonly sleep
with them.

Then suddenly the series ends, and you're back to being a
selection of disparate individuals. Without the link of a
mutual project, you realize that you never really had that
much in common.

With the murder solved, that was what had happened to
him and Sydnee.

He offered her another drink, but Jim Trace-Smith had
just bought a round, and a hand snaked out of the *If The Cap
Fits* group to pass her one. She asked if Charles was going to
have another, but he looked at his watch and said, no, he'd
better be going. She kissed him on the lips without passion,
thanked him again for everything, and with something like
relief coalesced once again with her group.

It was not yet seven, but Charles moved purposefully
towards the exit. Just as he got there, though, he encountered a fellow-actor who had just emerged from "the most
dreadful, but the most dreadful day in the studio on this
bloody bomb disposal soap opera". He was in desperate need
of a transfusion of alcohol. Surely Charles had time for one
little drink with him.

"Oh, all right," said Charles, looking at his watch again.
"Just one."

It was nearly ten to nine when he got to the Italian restaurant
in Hampstead. There was no sign of Frances.

"Hasn't she arrived?" he asked the proprietor. "She
would have asked for a table in the name of Paris."

"Oh yes, signor. The lady was here. She left about five
minutes ago."

"Did she leave any message?"

"No, signor. No message."